"*Why do you hate the Harkness family?*" *Phil snarled.*

"Everybody knows how much trouble they've. . .," Larry suddenly realized what he was saying was self-incriminating and he let his voice trail off.

"We can put fifty witnesses on the stand who will testify you swore to them you would get even with the Harkness family," Scott retorted, unmoved by Larry's whimpering tone.

"Tell us how you torched the place, Larry. It'll go easier for you," Phil explained sternly.

Larry's face whitened. His hands and shoulders began to tremble. *These guys are for real. I could go to the state pen in Deer Lodge for something I didn't do. I was able to plead temporary insanity as a minor when I shot Mr. Walker, but nobody will defend me now.*

Vanessa's innocent face flashed before him. *I can't let my little girl grow up knowing her daddy's in jail.* Larry pictured Libby's sweet face and long blond hair on their wedding day. He pictured her the day he saw her in the supermarket parking lot. . . .

"I want to talk with Bob Harkness. I know it would take an act of God for anyone to come to my rescue in such circumstances. But I have nowhere else to turn. Please let me try," Larry pleaded as tears streamed down his cheeks. Every fiber in his being cried for help and there was only this faint ray of hope.

ANN BELL, a librarian by profession, lives in Billings, Montana, with her attorney husband. Ann has worked as a teacher and librarian in schools in Iowa, Oregon, Guam, as well as Montana. Previously she has written numerous articles for Christian magazines and the books *Proving Yourself: A Study of James* and *Autumn Love*, book one in the "Rocky Bluff Chronicles."

Books by Ann Bell

HEARTSONG PRESENTS

HP66—Autumn Love

Contagious Love

Ann Bell

Rocky Bluff Chronicles: Book Two

Heartsong Presents

This book is dedicated to my mother, Frances Hartman, and to my late father, Walter Hartman, my two children, and my four stepchildren. I trust that our love is contagious to our grandchildren Ryan Orr, Vanessa Sanchez, and Michael Mishler.

A note from the Author:
I love to hear from my readers! You may correspond with me by writing:

Ann Bell
Author Relations
P.O. Box 719
Uhrichsville, OH 44683

ISBN 1-55748-562-3

CONTAGIOUS LOVE

PRINTED IN THE U.S.A.

one

"Hello, Crisis Center. May I help you?"

"I hope so," a frightened voice whispered. "I can't talk long. My husband is going to be back in a few minutes. He's been beating me. My eye is swelling so badly that I can hardly see."

Edith Dutton took a deep breath and whispered a quick prayer for wisdom. This was her first call at the Crisis Center after returning from her honeymoon, and in spite of her sixty-seven years the potential for serious consequences sent chills down her spine. "What do you think will happen when he gets back?"

"He left to buy more beer so it'll probably only get worse. I'm really scared. He told me that if I didn't have this house spotless by the time he got back he'd beat me bloody. I've really tried, but I've been sick lately. I'm always nauseated and can hardly keep any food down."

"We'll have to get you out of there right away. Do you have any friends or relatives where you'd be safe?"

"No. My mother died when I was twelve, and my dad and stepmother live in Iowa, but they wouldn't be able to help. I've been so busy with the baby that I haven't had time to make friends of my own."

"There are several local agencies that can help. In fact, we have a Spouse Abuse Shelter here in Rocky Bluff. Hurry and pack a few things for you and your baby, and I'll have the director of the shelter come and get you right away. Of course, the police will have to be notified."

"Do they have to be?" Terror vibrated through her words. "He'll really be mad then. I know they'll put him in jail because he's already on probation."

"Right now your safety and the safety of your baby is what's important. What's your name and where are you?"

"My name is Libby. . .Libby Reynolds. My baby's name is Vanessa. I'm at 2519 Frontage Road. Please hurry. I'm expecting him back any time and I haven't gotten everything done he told me to do."

"I'll call the police and they'll be there in just a few minutes," Edith assured her. "Now what's the name of your husband and what kind of car is he driving?"

Libby hesitated. *What will he do to me if I tell? If only I'd been a better wife maybe this wouldn't have happened.* The silence became penetrating. Finally she whispered. "He's driving a red Ford Maverick. His name is Larry Reynolds."

Edith's face whitened, her hands turned clammy. Her mind flashed back nearly three years. She again felt the terror of staring into the muzzle of a .38 Police Special in the hands of Larry Reynolds with her principal, Grady Walker, lying wounded at her feet. She had not seen Larry since that time and she had desperately tried to block those memories out of her mind.

Edith took a deep breath. *I have to keep my composure. This girl's life is in danger.*

"Libby, my name is Edith Harkness," she said, trying to keep her voice calm. "My husband and I will be there with the Director of the Spouse Abuse Center in fifteen minutes. Be waiting for us at the door."

Edith hurriedly hung up the phone, thankful that she had an extension of the Crisis Center line in her own home. "Roy," she shouted as she rushed to the coat closet beside the front door. "Get your coat. There's a young woman in serious danger."

Roy laid his newspaper on the end table and helped Edith with her coat before reaching for his own. As the director of the Crisis Center he was used to handling problems over the phone, but never had he seen his best counselor so intent to personally intervene in a case. "What's happened?" he queried, fearing for the health of his beloved bride.

"We've got to get Larry Reynolds's wife to the Spouse Abuse Shelter. He's been beating on her and then left to get more beer. She's scared to death and so am I. We can call Teresa from the car phone and tell her we'll stop by her house on our way to get Libby."

"I was afraid that boy would end up a menace to society," Roy said as they raced to the car. "A lot of people have tried to help him but he refused to listen to anyone. I bet he's going to be spending time in the state penitentiary in Deer Lodge before his life is over. I like to give people the benefit of the doubt, but with Larry I question if there is much hope for him."

Roy opened the left door of their Chrysler LeBaron for Edith and then hurried around the car and slid behind the wheel. "I'm sure glad we have such a flexible spouse abuse director as Teresa. She's done so much for this community."

Edith picked up the car phone and dialed 789-2540 and waited. *What if she's not home?* she worried with each passing ring. Suddenly the ringing stopped.

"Hello."

Edith breathed a sigh of relief. "Teresa, thank goodness you're home. Roy and I are on our way over to get you. Larry Reynolds's wife just called the Crisis Center and he's been beating her. After my dreadful experience with him I'm afraid for her life. I told her we'd take her and the baby directly to the Spouse Abuse Shelter."

"I'll get my coat and be watching for you," Teresa assured her. "Sonya, one of our best volunteers, is staying at the shelter tonight so she'll have an extra bed and crib waiting for her. Have you called the police yet?"

"That's my next call."

Roy looked over at his trembling wife. The streetlights magnified the tension in her face. Those same wrinkles that he had watched gradually fade after Edith's near fatal heart attack were now spreading across her face. The same young man who had caused enough fear in the calm home economics teacher of Rocky Bluff High School to raise her blood pressure to dangerous heights was again threatening Edith's serenity and the life of his own wife and child.

Edith quickly dialed 9-1-1.

"Emergency services. May I help you?" a confident voice said.

"Hello, this is Edith Dutton. I'd like to report a case of domestic violence with the wife's life in imminent danger. My husband and I, along with Teresa Lennon from the Spouse Abuse Center, are on our way to get her, but he's been drinking and we could run into problems. Could we have a police officer meet us there right away?"

"Don't worry, they'll be right there. Where are you going?"

"We're on our way to 2519 Frontage Road to get Libby Reynolds," Edith explained as she tried to keep her voice under control. "Her husband, Larry Reynolds, just left to get more beer and threatened to beat her more when he got home."

"You said his name was Larry Reynolds." The dispatcher's tone indicated he was familiar with the name.

"Yes," Edith gasped.

"Do you know what kind of a car he might be driving? Maybe they will be able to stop him before he gets home."

"Libby said he was driving a red Ford Maverick. She didn't say what year."

"That information is extremely helpful. I'll have the police on their way. Now be careful," the dispatcher warned. "If Larry is any place in the vicinity when you get there don't approach the house until the police arrive."

Edith's hand trembled as she hung up the car phone. She was torn by her desire to help Libby and her fear of having to face Larry Reynolds again. She visualized that same .38 Police Special pointed at a young, frightened woman and knew what she had to do.

Just then Roy turned their Chrysler from Main onto Sixth Street. He immediately discerned a trim figure hurrying toward the curb. He steered to the edge of the street and stopped. Teresa wasted no time in opening the door and sliding into the back seat.

"Hi. Thanks for taking such a personal interest in this case. It could be real touchy. Were you able to get hold of the police?"

"Oh yes," Edith replied. "I called them as soon as I hung up from talking with you. The dispatcher said she would send a squad car there immediately. It looks like Larry will be spending a lot more time behind bars."

"I would think so," Roy responded dryly. "The last time he pled temporary insanity and only spent six months in a mental hospital. He obviously didn't learn anything from that. I've heard he's been involved in a all kinds of fights at the bars after he's had a few drinks under his belt. I hope we don't have to deal with that."

"No," Edith assured him. "The dispatcher advised us that if Larry is around we are not to go near the house until the police arrive. They will handle the situation."

As Roy turned onto the Frontage Road a red Maverick sped around them and nearly hit a parked car. The trio gasped.

"Better hurry," Edith directed. "I want to be waiting in the car in case Libby runs from the house with nowhere to go."

As Roy increased the pressure on the accelerator he spotted blue and red flashing lights three blocks behind them and gaining on them quickly. They all breathed a sigh of relief as Roy pulled to the right and the patrol car sped around them.

"Thank you, Lord," Edith whispered as they followed the authorities to the Reynolds residence.

"Boy, am I glad to see them," Teresa gasped. "I've been in tough predicaments before with domestic abuse, but never this bad."

Sergeant Philip Mooney and Officer Scott Packwood stopped in front of 2519 Frontage Road and stepped from their patrol car. Having recognized the Dutton car as they had sped past them they waited on the curb for the fast approaching Chrysler.

In the glimmer of the streetlight Edith recognized one of the officers. *I'm sure glad Phil's on duty now,* she mused. *He did such a good job handling Larry three years ago.*

Roy pulled up behind the police car and the threesome hurried toward the waiting officers.

"I'm glad you're here," Sergeant Mooney greeted.

"Depending on how much Larry's been drinking we could have a real problem on our hands. I don't want to put his wife or child in danger. He's on parole so he's not suppose to own a firearm, but we don't want to take any chances. At this point he could use anything as a weapon, even his fists. I'm hoping there's some way we can talk the wife and baby out of the house before we have to confront Larry."

"Since I was the one Libby spoke to, maybe if I went to the door alone as a friend I could get Libby and the baby outside without upsetting Larry any more than necessary."

"Edith, I can't ask you to do that," Sergeant Mooney protested weakly. "We're the ones who are paid to take the risks, not you."

"Phil, I faced Larry once with a loaded gun and God gave me the strength. If He could protect me three years ago He can do it tonight."

"I'll admit that method might be least likely to cause Larry to fly into a rage. Are you sure you're up to it?"

Roy was filled with trepidation as he surveyed his wife's strained face. His love and admiration for her escalated with each passing moment. He wondered how he had ever survived the long lonely years of widowhood without her. And now the thought of her voluntarily putting her life on the line for someone she had never met was nearly overwhelming.

Edith looked at Roy for assurance. Their eyes met, but no words escaped their lips for several seconds. Finally, Roy nodded his head up and down.

"I have the best protection in the world," Edith replied bravely. "And with everyone here for backup I'll try my best."

"Don't forget we'll be hiding in the bushes with

revolvers drawn if you have any problems," Sergeant Mooney responded as he and Officer Packwood moved toward the shadows of the bushes surrounding the house.

Roy squeezed Edith's hand. She took a deep breath and walked slowly toward the front door. She could hear shouting within, but could not make out the words. Hesitantly she reached for the doorbell.

"Who's there?" a gruff voice shouted.

"I'm a friend of Libby's. I wanted to come by and say hello. I haven't seen her for several weeks."

"She's busy now and doesn't have time to see anyone."

"I'll only be a minute. Please tell her she has a friend."

Edith could hear muffled sobs behind the closed doors. "No. . .wait a minute," a female voice cried. "Please don't go away. I need your help. You sound like the woman I talked with on the phone tonight."

"What do you mean were you wasting your time talking on the phone tonight? You were suppose to be cleaning this pig sty while I was gone," the male voice growled.

"I. . . I'm sorry. I was just lonely. Please let me talk to her for just one minute. I promise I'll not call anyone again."

"You don't need to see anyone. Do I have to blacken your other eye to get you to understand that?"

Suddenly baby Vanessa began to cry. The entire household was a mass of crying and shouting. Time was suspended as the male curses behind the thin walls increased. Slowly the door opened. A young emaciated woman with swollen eyes and bruises appeared in the doorway holding a screaming baby. Edith grabbed her arm and dragged her down the three steps with a husky male figure close behind.

"Get back here you worthless, no-good piece of. . ."

Larry shouted. His voice trailed off as a glimmer of recognition spread across his face. He grabbed the poker from beside the fireplace as he followed his wife through the open door. "What are you doing with my wife? You messed up my life once before while I was in high school. I won't let you do that again."

With revolvers drawn, Sergeant Mooney and Office Packwood came between the two women and their assailant. "Larry Reynolds, you're under arrest for violating probation and assault and battery."

While the arresting officials were reading Larry his Miranda Rights, Teresa led Libby and the crying baby to the Dutton vehicle. Although she had cared for many troubled families throughout the years, she always felt ill-prepared for the pain that they shared. She wrapped a blanket around the sobbing woman and put her arms around her. Not a word was spoken as the sobs subsided and Libby relaxed with her head on Teresa's shoulder. All energy and emotion seemed to be drained from the frightened woman.

"Our first stop will be the emergency room," Teresa explained gently. "We need to have your injuries checked."

"I'll be okay," Libby sobbed. "Besides I can't go to the hospital. I don't have any insurance."

"Don't let insurance stand in the way of your health," Teresa replied. "I'll be able to help you get financial assistance for medical care."

"But what'll I do after they've patched me up? If I come back here he'll only beat me again."

"The police will have him busy in jail for a long time tonight. After Larry is gone we'll come back and get your things. Has the baby been hurt in anyway?"

"Oh, no. She's just scared." Libby's voice trembled.

"She's the apple of her daddy's eye. He said if I ever left him he'd get custody of Vanessa 'cause he could prove I was an unfit mother."

The young woman watched as the officers handcuffed her husband and placed him in the back of the patrol car. "The only reason why I've stayed with him was because of Vanessa. I take really good care of her. Do you think he'd be able to take her away from me?"

"Of course not. He's just using that to scare you. You won't have to worry about him bothering you again," Teresa assured her. "I think the officers have plans for him for a long time."

"But I don't want to be the one that caused him to go to jail. After all, it wasn't all his fault. I should have had the house cleaned up when he got home today, but I've been so sick lately."

"No one deserves to be treated the way you've been. Your immediate need is medical care, a good hot meal, and a warm bed. We'll begin working on the rest of your life tomorrow."

"It's strange," Libby sighed. "I know I can't keep living with Larry like this. However, sometimes I still feel a spark of love, in spite of everything he's done."

"Libby, love is complex and multifaceted. Tomorrow will be soon enough to begin evaluating your feelings toward Larry. Right now it's time to get you to the emergency room."

While the police officers were leading Larry to the police car and Teresa was comforting Libby in the back seat of the car, Edith and Roy clung to each other under the reflection of the street light. Edith laid her head upon Roy's chest. Her breathing was rapid and her heart raced. "Edith, you're one brave lady. I've never seen anyone as self-sacrificing as you. But are you going to be okay?"

"A cup of hot tea and a good night's sleep will go a long way." Edith's words sounded strong, but the quiver in her voice betrayed her weak heart.

"While Libby is being examined in the emergency room I think we better have your blood pressure checked."

"I hate to admit that I'm not as strong as I used to be, but I guess you're right. I don't want to go through heart surgery again. I have too much to live for now." Her eyes twinkled as she lightly brushed her lips across his. "I have the best husband in the world," she whispered as the pair walked to their car hand in hand.

two

"Mom, I just heard the news and I came over as soon as I could," Bob Harkness said as he walked into his mother's kitchen. "It's all over town."

"Word travels fast in a little town," Edith smiled. "I was just getting ready to call you at the store when I saw your car in the drive. Now that you're here, would you like a cup of coffee?"

"I'd love it," Bob replied as he reached for a mug in the cupboard over the coffeepot. "With your increasing reputation for bravery you're quickly becoming the community folk hero."

Edith chuckled as she admired her son's muscular shoulders. Years of work at the family hardware store had developed his physical strength. Edith thought back to the days when he first returned to Rocky Bluff to manage Harkness Hardware Store after her first husband, George, died. She had worked as the bookkeeper while her husband ordered the merchandise and waited on customers. Feeling inept at managing the entire business without him, she asked Bob to manage it for her while she returned to teaching.

Bob pulled up a chair at the kitchen table. "Mom, you're one brave lady. You always put the needs of others ahead of your own. I hope that experience last night didn't put too much strain on your heart."

"I feel perfectly fine today. Knowing that Libby is being cared for at the shelter and Larry is in jail gives me a great deal of peace."

"I don't think Larry will be in jail long." Bob hesitated as he surveyed the dark circles under his mother's eyes. "The rumor on the street is that bail will probably be set at five thousand dollars. I saw his parents go into the bank first thing this morning so my guess is that they'll take out another mortgage on the ranch in order to post his bond."

Edith stared out the kitchen window at the barren elm tree in the backyard. She well understood the pain Larry's family must be feeling. "I'm sure his parents must be heartbroken. I know they were crushed after the trouble Larry got into three years ago."

"From my observation they appeared to be so ashamed that they quit going to church and community events for several months. It wasn't until their pastor and church people rallied behind them that we began seeing them in Rocky Bluff again," Bob replied. "I don't think they realized how much the community hurt for them. The town knew it was Larry's decision to pull the gun on the principal, not theirs, but until people began articulating their feelings to them they had no way of knowing."

"In a way I understand what they must be going through. Although it's the child's decisions, a parent is programmed from the time they hear the first cry to feel they are responsible. I guess I've never quite gotten over feeling responsible for you and Jean, in spite of the fact that you both now have your own families."

"Mom, I wish you wouldn't try to carry my burdens. I'm the only one responsible for the times when I mess up. I'm just glad that we have a forgiving Lord and you have a forgiving husband."

"I have to agree with both those statements," Edith

replied as she reached across the table and patted her son's hand. "Plus I have to add that I'm also thankful for a repentant son who was willing to own up to his mistakes. Without that I would never have had this beautiful marriage to enjoy during my later years."

Edith's mind drifted back to the time of Bob's opposition to her relationship with Roy. He'd been more interested in preserving his portion of the family inheritance than concerned for his mother's well-being or happiness. The tragic part was that Bob had involved Roy's mentally handicapped son, Pete, in his scheme to keep them from marrying. That scheme culminated in a fatal car accident that left Pete dead and Bob in the hospital.

"Bob, what you've done with your life since the accident is nearly miraculous, especially the work you've done to help the local boys club. The parents of those kids appreciate it very much."

"I want to help the kids enter adulthood with the right values, decision-making abilities, and proficiency in handling stress. I know I had the right values taught to me, but I never saw how important they were until I destroyed another person's life."

Edith sighed. "Larry Reynolds had the right values taught to him, but sad to say he never learned them. I hope something can be done to help him before he destroys his life and the lives of those around him."

"If there's any way I can help him I sure would like to try." Bob refilled his coffee cup before he continued. "I need another challenge to keep my mind off my difficulties at the store. Things are really getting tough."

"Are you having problems getting your shipments on time? I know that was one of your father's biggest concerns."

"I wish it were that simple. This recession is taking its toll on our sales. With farm prices so low, farmers and ranchers can't afford new equipment. All of them seem to be fixing what they have and trying to make do to get through another season."

Worry spread across Edith's face. "How bad is it?"

"I have three large payments to major vendors next week and I'm not sure how I'm going to pay even one of them. I'll probably have to go talk to our friendly banker and take out a loan. I hate to take on more indebtedness with the economy this shaky, but I don't see any other way to handle it."

"Maybe if you talk to the vendors they'll accept partial payment for a month or two."

"I tried that. They said I have to pay in full or they will be forced to cut off all sales to me until the entire bill is paid. They are key suppliers; I can't be without their products."

"I guess you don't have any other choice than to see Rick at First National. He always treated us fairly during the recession of the late seventies."

Bob rose from the kitchen table, rinsed out his cup, and set it in the sink. "I better get back to the store. I told Nancy I wouldn't be gone long. She's been such an encouragement for me. I don't know how I'd ever have gotten along without her."

❧

Edith spent the remainder of the morning reading the *Rocky Bluff Herald*. The silence of the empty house was relaxing as she stretched out in her favorite chair, and it wasn't long before she dozed off with the paper across her chest. Promptly at twelve o'clock she was awakened when the back door banged.

"Is that you, Roy?"

Roy wiped his feet on the doormat, crossed the kitchen and living room with several long strides, and planted a kiss on his drowsy wife's forehead. "How's my lovely bride? I hope you've had a chance to rest from your exciting evening last night."

"Hi, dear. I guess you caught me napping," Edith sleepily replied. "I'm doing great. Bob came over a little while this morning. It seems the whole town is talking about Larry's arrest."

"I'm sure they are. By the way, while I was working at the Crisis Center this morning Teresa called. She was concerned how you were doing and didn't want to bother you in case you were resting."

"I'm glad everyone's concerned, but people worry too much about me," Edith assured him. "I'm fine. There's not much the Lord and I can't handle together. Did she say how Libby was doing?"

"Except for being covered with bruises, she'll be okay. However, Teresa would like you to call her sometime this afternoon." Roy paused a moment and then chuckled. "I think she needs some of your motherly advice."

"She's a good social worker, I'm sure I can't tell her anything that she doesn't already know."

"I take it last night's experience really unnerved her. She asked me to let her know the next time we have a training program for volunteers at the Crisis Center. She believes that training would be invaluable for her."

"It would be good for anybody," Edith reminded him, as she remembered how waluable her training had been. "Textbook learning can only do so much. It might help if Teresa spent a few weekend evenings answering the crisis line. You get a totally different image of life in Rocky

Bluff than from what you observe on Main Street during the daytime."

"That's true. Few people realize the heartache that goes on behind closed doors." Roy glanced toward the kitchen clock. "Edith, I bet you haven't had anything to eat yet. Why don't you let me fix you a tuna salad sandwich?"

"That sounds good. While you're doing that I'll warm up a can of tomato soup."

After lunch Edith dialed 789-2540 and waited.

"Hello."

"Hello, Teresa. This is Edith. How are you doing today?"

"I'm fine, but more importantly, how are you? You had quite a fright last night."

Edith smiled. "My blood pressure is back to normal and I had a good rest this morning. How's Libby doing?"

"Outside of being black-and-blue she's going to be okay physically. However, I'm really concerned about her emotional stability. She bears many of the classic symptoms of spousal abuse. Her self-esteem is at rock bottom and she seems to think she deserved it."

"That's too bad," Edith responded as she imagined the pain Libby must be experiencing. "However, even though it looks pretty bleak now, nothing is too difficult for God to heal."

"That's what impressed her the most about you. . . . Your faith in God is unshakable." Teresa hesitated. "That's the area I feel the most limited to talk about and Libby kept asking questions. I was wondering if you'd have some free time when I could bring her over so you could answer some of her questions."

"I promised my grandchildren they could come over and play Monopoly this afternoon. Jay and Dawn are hard to turn down. Could we make it tomorrow afternoon?"

Teresa giggled. "I didn't think kids played Monopoly anymore."

"They do at my house. I'm not into video games, yet."

"Edith, I'm taking Libby some disposable diapers this afternoon. I'll see if tomorrow will be okay with her."

"I'm looking forward to meeting with her. If there's anything more I can do to help, please let me know."

"You've done more than your share. However, I get the feeling Libby is going to be turning to you more and more. She was very impressed with the love you and Roy have for each other and can't understand why she and Larry can't have the same."

Promptly at two o'clock the next afternoon Teresa's Chevy Capri stopped in front of the Dutton residence. Edith watched out of her front window as Libby unfastened Vanessa from the car seat and joined Teresa on the sidewalk. Her heart sank as she observed the dejected slump in the young woman's walk. *Poor self-esteem is written all over her,* Edith mused.

"Welcome. Do come in out of the cold," Edith greeted as she flung open the door before Teresa had a chance to reach for the doorbell.

The two women stepped into the entryway. "Edith, it's good to see you again," Teresa said as she automatically wiped her shoes on the doormat. "I'd love to stay but I have a few errands to run. I'll be back in about an hour. You two have a nice visit."

"I'm sure we will," Edith responded as she opened the hall closet and took out a coat hanger for Libby. "I'll have the coffee pot on when you get back."

Teresa shut the door quietly behind her as Edith turned

her attention to the baby in her mother's arms. "Libby, may I hold Vanessa while you take your coat off?"

Libby handed the baby to the older woman, hung her coat in the open closet, and glanced around the room. "You have a lovely home. It has so much warmth and charm. I don't think I'll ever have a decent home of my own. I can't even keep a husband."

Edith gulped. Right away she was searching for the right words. "Libby, what happened last night was not your fault. Larry has never been able to handle stress. He's like the person who's angry with his boss and feels he can't do anything about it so he takes it out on his innocent dog when he gets home."

"Yeah, I know what you mean," Libby sighed. "Every once in a while I see Larry kicking our dog, Ralph. The poor thing just looks up at him with his big brown eyes that say, 'What did I do to you?'"

"I'm afraid Larry treats you the same way he treats Ralph. Beating on you is merely a way for him to relieve stress."

"But I so wanted our marriage to work." Libby bit her lip. "I did everything I could think of to make him happy but it still wasn't enough."

"I'm sure you did," Edith sympathized. Sensing the conversation was about to become intense, Edith motioned toward the door at the side of the room. "Let's go to the kitchen; I seem to have my best conversations around my kitchen table."

"Vanessa is acting sleepy. Do you have a place I can lay her down?"

Edith smiled as she remembered other young mothers such as Beth Slater who found their way to her kitchen table while their babies slept on a blanket folded up in the corner of the living room. She reached into her closet and took out a faded quilt. "Vanessa should be comfortable in this corner and we can watch her from the kitchen," she said as she spread the quilt on the floor.

While the baby slept peacefully the two women sipped on their coffee. "Libby, it's very natural that you have mixed feelings toward Larry. You have good reason to be angry for how much he hurt you both physically and emotionally. I'm sure the emotional pain is far worse than the physical abuse you took."

Libby took a Kleenex from her purse. "It was awful. He would claim he loved me one minute and be shouting at me and insulting me the next. He was always angry about something."

"Honey, the most important thing you'll need to do in your relationship with Larry is try to understand what is actually your problem and what is his," Edith comforted with her typical maternal instinct.

"It just seems like one massive problem to me, not part his and part mine."

Edith surveyed the tear-filled eyes of her young guest. "It will probably seem that way for a while, but little by little you'll look at a particular situation and say, 'That's Larry's problem and I can't do anything about it'. Other times you'll be able to say, 'That's my problem and I can do something about it.'"

Libby thought a moment, sighed, and then smiled. "I guess you're right. I really can't help it when he forgets where he left his tools when he's fixing the car. But somehow I've been led to believe that it's my responsibility to always have everything available for him whenever he wants them."

"You're learning fast," Edith assured her as she poured

another cup of coffee. "You're off to a good start and there are many great things ahead for you."

The hour passed quickly as Libby unloaded her fears and doubts to the retired home economics teacher. It wasn't long before Teresa was ringing the doorbell. At the first buzz Vanessa awoke with a whimper as Edith went to answer the door.

"Teresa, do come in. We still have a little coffee left in the pot," Edith greeted as she motioned for the social worker to enter.

"Thanks. I'm sure you two had a good visit. I'm sorry it took longer than I expected. The traffic was terrible and the lines were long. The usual routine."

"No problem. We did have a good visit. I know it's difficult for Libby at the shelter without transportation, but do you think someone could bring her to see me every two or three days? We have so much we want to talk about."

"That shouldn't be a problem. We have a good crew of volunteers, especially Sonya and Patricia. Most of them have been right where Libby is today. They know what it's like to be abused and are anxious to help others in the same situations."

Teresa followed Edith into the kitchen. "I will take you up on your offer for a cup of coffee," she said as she pulled out a chair and sat down. "There is something we need to discuss with Libby."

The young mother picked up her baby from her makeshift bed in the corner and followed the others to the kitchen. A frightened, bewildered look spread across her face. *This must be serious. I must be in a lot of trouble now,* she thought.

Sensing her concern, Teresa reached over and patted

her shoulder. "Relax. Everything's working out for the best. You just have a decision to make."

Libby gave a weak smile as she returned to the chair she had just left. "I don't know if I'm up to making a rational decision now or not."

"We're here to help you," Edith assured her as she refilled Libby's cup.

Teresa took a deep breath while she studied the frightened girl's face. "I saw Sergeant Mooney this afternoon. He'd just been out to the shelter to talk with you, but of course you were gone. Anyway, he needs to know by tonight whether you want to press assault and battery charges against Larry."

Libby's face whitened. "If I press charges he'll try to take Vanessa away from me."

Teresa gulped. "Even though he'll probably be out on bail in a few days there's no chance that he could get custody at this point since he has violated parole," she assured Libby. "Vanessa is still nursing and must have her mother."

Silence enveloped the room as Libby remained deep in thought. "I think I still love him; I don't want him to go to jail."

"You would not be the one who sends him to jail, that's a decision for the judge," Edith assured her. "Larry knew drinking alcoholic beverages was against his parole. That was his decision and not yours."

"But what good would it accomplish if I did press charges?"

"The decision is entirely yours," Teresa assured her. "The important thing is that you will never again be abused. No woman deserves that kind of treatment."

Libby again paused before she spoke. "Larry doesn't

know how to control his temper. I wonder if there is some way he could learn how to do that without having to go to jail."

"The mental health clinic does provide training in stress management. We might suggest that Larry be required to attend," the social worker explained. "But again, it's the judge's decision."

"I'm really scared to live with him. . . but I don't want to press charges. . .I don't want to go back home, but I don't have anywhere else to go."

"You and Vanessa can stay at the shelter for up to a month. During that time we'll see that you find a place to stay. We'll help you get government assistance and obtain training or employment."

Libby gasped as a smile spread across her face. "You mean you'd do all that for me? I don't deserve it."

"Of course you do," Edith quickly replied. "The only requirement is that after others have helped you it will be your turn to pass it on."

"That's right," Teresa agreed. "All the volunteers of the Spouse Abuse Center once came to us as victims. Many of the Crisis Center volunteers once struggled with difficult problems themselves. It's their way of passing help on to others."

"If they can do it so can I." Libby snuggled her baby to her chest. "However, I don't think I could live with myself if I pressed charges against Vanessa's father. As long as he never hurts me again I think I'll be able to forgive him."

three

"Good afternoon. May I help you?" Bob asked as he approached a middle-aged couple standing in the middle of a section of snowblowers.

"Hello, Mr. Harkness. I'm just pricing snowblowers. Mine gave out during the last blizzard and I can't decide whether to have it fixed or buy a new one."

Bob gulped as he recognized Donald and Frances Reynolds. *I wanted to find a way to help Larry and here I am face-to-face with his parents. I hope I'll be able to encourage them instead of hurting them any more than they already are.*

"Mr. Reynolds, now is a good time to buy. We have a mid-winter sale on all winter equipment."

Donald silently walked through the row of snowblowers and examined the price tags. "This one's not bad. Could I buy it on time? Things are kind of tight at the ranch right now."

Bob's mind raced. *I'm not making any money at all with this sale and selling anything on credit only makes it worse, but I've got to turn over this inventory in order to get at least a little cash flow.*

"How about seventy-five a month until it's paid off at 9 percent?"

Donald rubbed his chin and then looked at Frances. She nodded in the affirmative.

"Mr. Harkness, I do appreciate you doing this for us. Things are pretty tough right now," Frances said weakly.

"Do call me Bob," the store owner insisted. "I sympathize with what your family is going through. If there is anything I can do to help please let me know."

"Your family has already done so much to help. I know Larry doesn't see it this way, but your mother has stepped in twice and kept him from getting in even more trouble. If she hadn't protected Libby last night who knows what Larry would have done to her."

"I'll admit my mother is one brave lady, but we both believe that Larry has a lot of potential. Hopefully, he can work out his problems before he destroys himself."

"I'm glad that someone else believes in him," Frances smiled. "Most people act like we're crazy to take another mortgage on the ranch to bail him out of jail. Even Rick at First National thought long and hard before he signed the papers, but we just can't give up on him despite what he's done. After all, he is still our son."

"With God's help anyone can change no matter what they've done," Bob assured her. "I wish there were some way I could befriend Larry. I'm sure he feels the entire world is against him now."

"He's felt that way since his senior year in high school," Donald replied. "After his scholarship to Montana A&M was canceled because of smoking pot after the state basketball tournament, his entire world seemed to fall apart."

"We're going to be picking him up from the jail later this afternoon. We'll tell him about your offer. I'm sure he'll appreciate it."

That afternoon Frances and Donald Reynolds walked into the Little Big Horn County Courthouse in Rocky Bluff and went directly to the Clerk of Court's Office with a five thousand dollar check in their hands. The paperwork for Larry's bail was processed quickly and within a few minutes the Reynoldses were face-to-face with their son.

Larry's face was tense and pale as he approached his parents. "Hello, Mom. . . Dad. Thanks for posting bond. That jail is definitely not a nice place to be. I didn't sleep all night. There were all kinds of weird things going on. I don't deserve to be in a place like that."

"Those were pretty serious charges brought against you," Donald reminded him gently. "Sergeant Mooney doesn't take lightly to parole violation. I guess you're fortunate that Libby didn't press assault and battery charges against you."

"Son, why don't you come back to the ranch and stay with us until your case comes to trial? The fresh, clean air will do you good." Frances choked back her tears.

Larry remained silent as the threesome walked slowly to the family Bronco. They felt eyes from every store around the town square peering out at them. Larry slid into the backseat as his father started the engine of the four-wheel drive. "Going home with you sounds like a good idea. I can't stand this stinking town any longer. Let's go by my house and I'll get some of my clothes and Ralph. I'm sure Ryan would like to help care for him."

Donald smiled as he watched his older son's face in the rearview mirror. "Your little brother will be glad to do that. He's always thought Ralph was the most intelligent dog in the world and he's wanted to spend enough time with him to teach him to do tricks."

"Before I forget to tell you," Frances began hesitantly. "We stopped in Harkness Hardware Store earlier today to get a new snowblower. Bob Harkness said to tell you if there's anything he can do to help, you let him know."

"Humfff," Larry scowled as he slammed his fist against

the seat. "I wouldn't accept help from him if he was the last person on earth. Because of his mother I've spent time in jail twice. That entire family is my enemy, not someone I'd want to be friends with."

The Reynoldses finished their drive to the younger man's home in silence. Words could not express the confused emotions they were each feeling. Larry hurriedly packed his clothes, tools, stereo, and TV. As he was loading the Bronco he noticed the two dog dishes on the back stoop. *Good grief, Ralph hasn't had anything to eat or drink for twenty-four hours.*

"Ralph!!! Here Ralph!!!" Larry picked up the half-empty bag of dog food from the back porch and carried it to his father's car. "Where could that dumb dog be?" He glanced toward the garage and there was his mixed-variety mutt slithering toward him with his tail between his legs.

"Hello, there old buddy. I bet you're kind of thirsty." Larry patted his mangy dog and put some water in his dish from the outside water spigot.

"Dad, do you and Mom want to go on ahead of me? I'll follow you in my car. I want to give Ralph a chance to eat something first."

An hour later Larry pulled his Maverick into the familiar homestead. Ryan ran outside to greet him. Larry had never noticed before how much his little brother had grown to look like him since he'd gotten into junior high. "Hi," Ryan shouted. "Do you have Ralph with you?"

"I sure do," Larry answered as he alighted from his car with Ralph close on his heels. "I sure do. In fact I have a deal I want to make with you. If you'll promise to take good care of him, I'll let you have him. I'm going to be too busy trying to get my family back."

"Hey, thanks! That's great!" Ryan exclaimed. Then he stopped and looked at his older brother with puzzlement. "What do you mean you want to get your family back? I thought they threw you in the slammer for beating your wife."

"Just for your information, little brother, I still love her and the baby, and I'm going to get them back, regardless of what I have to do."

"Boy, that's a strange way to show love."

"There's a lot of things you'll never understand. There's two things I'm going to do. . ." Larry paused as if he were talking more to himself than to his brother. "I'm going to get my family back and I'm going to get even with the Harkness family."

Ryan's face whitened as he saw his brother in a totally different light. "But you can't do that. Jay's my best friend."

Late the next week Bob stopped at his mother's house on his way home from work. Roy, Edith, and Bob exchanged pleasantries and made themselves comfortable in the living room before Bob came to the point of his visit.

"Well. . . the worst has happened," Bob faltered before continuing. "Rick turned down my loan. He said it wasn't anything personal, but because of the recession and low farm prices I'm no longer a good credit risk."

Edith looked stunned. "This is the first time in history Harkness Hardware has been disapproved for credit . . . but then, it is the first time in history that the farm economy has been this bad."

"The farmers are really hurting. The only major piece of equipment I've sold all month was a snowblower to Donald Reynolds. But I had to sell it on credit, so it didn't help my cash flow at all. On top of my three main vendors screaming at me for money, I have a large insurance premium due next month. I just don't know what I'm going to do. I have to maintain fire insurance or my entire mortgage becomes due."

Wrinkles began to deepen on Edith's face. "The only thing I can think of is to pray," Edith replied. "There has to be a way out of this, but I'm afraid I don't have any easy answer to your dilemma."

The trio stared out the window in silence for several minutes before Roy tried to move the conversation to a more pleasant subject. "How's Jay adjusting to junior high this year? I can't believe he's grown as much as he has in the last few months."

The topic of his two children, Jay and Dawn, was usually enough to bring a smile to Bob's face and provoke several minutes of bragging of their latest accomplishments, but all he could say was, "That's the sad part. That store is the only means I have to support those kids and it won't be much longer before they'll be looking at going to college. Nancy may have to get a job outside of keeping the store books just to support the family. It really hurts my pride to even consider that."

To help reduce the gloom that settled over the Duttons' living room, Bob succumbed to Roy's lead and began talking about the children. Anything to keep from thinking about the "what ifs" of life.

Every other day either Sonya or Patricia would bring Libby to Edith's home and then leave for an hour-and-a-half before returning to take her back to the shelter. Libby and Edith's conversations covered everything from Libby's early life, parenthood, her relationship with Larry, faith in God, and the love and forgiveness offered through Jesus

Christ. No subject was off limits for discussion.

"I've been at the shelter for nearly three weeks now and I feel I'm over the hump and can begin looking for an apartment," Libby confided to Edith as she balanced Vanessa on her knee. "Teresa has helped me apply for welfare and we are looking into different programs so that I can support myself and Vanessa."

"I'm glad to hear you're so optimistic," Edith replied. "Since you began to realize how much Christ loves you, your self-esteem has skyrocketed. I'm sure you'll go far in life."

"I still kind of wish it could be with Larry, but I'm never going to let myself be abused again."

Edith poured Libby and herself another cup of coffee. "You're being very wise. Before you can have a successful marriage both parties have to be emotionally and spiritually healed. One person cannot do it by themselves." Just then the doorbell rang. Edith hurried across the living room and opened the door. Sonya was beaming from ear to ear.

"Come in, Sonya. You look like you're bursting with good news."

"I am," the young woman replied as she stepped into the entryway. "Libby is still here, isn't she?"

"Oh yes, we were just starting our second cup of coffee. Would you care to join us?"

"I'd love to."

Sonya handed her coat to Edith who quickly hung it in the hall closet. The young woman followed Edith into her kitchen where Libby was sitting with a puzzled look on her face.

"Sonya, you're back early."

"Yes, and I have some great news," Sonya replied as

she made herself comfortable at the end of the table. "I just ran into a friend of mine, Pam Claiborne, and she is getting married next week and will be moving out of her apartment. She has a real cute place over on Ash Street. It's kind of small, but it would be just perfect for you and Vanessa."

Libby's eyes lit up, then she hesitated. "It sounds terrific, but I can't afford even the first month's rent, much less a deposit."

"This apartment complex is approved for Section Eight, which means the amount of rent you pay is based on your income. I'm sure we can work something out. Pam can show you the place today if you'd like."

"Libby," Edith inserted, "our church has a fund to help those who have special needs. While you and Sonya go look at the place I'll give Pastor Rhodes a call and see if he can help. You can repay the fund when you get back on your feet."

"That's a great idea," Sonya said. "Edith, would you mind if I use your phone to give Pam a call? I want to tell her we'll be right over."

Sonya's conversation with Pam was short. The two young women slipped into their coats and Libby hurriedly put Vanessa in her snowsuit and grabbed her diaper bag. This could be a major turning point in her life.

The following Saturday the young adult's group from the church gathered to help Libby move into her new apartment. When Libby returned to her former home on Frontage Road she was relieved to discover that Larry had not taken the furniture. Mixed feelings flooded her. *Is this a new beginning in my life, or just the end of a marriage? I have no choice but to go through with this. I know I can't afford the rent on this house any longer and it's obvious that Larry just walked away and abandoned it.*

At the end of the day tears filled Libby's eyes as she surveyed her new living room cluttered with boxes. "How can I thank you for helping me this way?" she told the small band of new friends.

Patricia smiled. "We've all been in situations where we need another's help. This group has helped me move at least twice. We meet every Wednesday night for study and old-fashioned fun. I hope you'll be able to join us. We even provide babysitters for those who need them."

"I. . .I don't know what to say," Libby stammered. "Nobody has ever helped me before. You've all been so good to me. I'd love to come."

"Good. I'll pick you up around seven o'clock Wednesday," Patricia replied.

The next two weeks went quickly for Libby as she unpacked boxes, hung pictures, and settled into her new apartment. Her visits with Edith became less frequent.

Late Friday night, the phone rang at the Dutton residence. "Hello," Edith greeted as she pushed her gray-flecked, black hair away from her ear.

"Hello, Edith. This is Libby. I'm sorry to call so late, but I didn't know what else to do. I'm really scared."

"What's the matter, Libby?"

"Larry must have found out where I live because he's been in front of the apartment in his red Maverick all afternoon. When I walked to the grocery store he followed me. He waited outside and followed me home."

Wrinkles appeared in Edith's forehead. "Did he say anything to you?"

"All he said was, 'I'm going to get Vanessa.' I won't let anyone take my baby away from me."

"Libby, Montana has just passed some very strong

antistalking laws. Is Larry still in front of your house?"

Libby pulled the drapes back a few inches. "Yes, he's still there. I wonder if he'll ever leave."

"I'll give Sergeant Mooney a call and see if he can come and have him move on. Also, tomorrow you may need to have a restraining order drawn up to keep Larry from bothering you and Vanessa," Edith replied.

"How do I do that? I can't afford an attorney."

"We can give Legal Services a call tomorrow. They take cases for those who can't afford regular legal fees. Maybe Sonya or Patricia could give you a ride. I'll talk to you tomorrow about that. Right now we better hang up so I can call Sergeant Mooney. Call me in a few minutes if Larry is still there. In the meantime, make sure all your windows and doors are locked."

four

A Rocky Bluff police car cruised quietly down Ash Street toward the Forest Grove Apartments. Sure enough, a red Ford Maverick with a man slouched behind the wheel was parked in front of the complex. Sergeant Mooney stopped his car behind the Ford and cautiously approached the driver.

"Larry, would you mind getting out of your car and talking with me?" Sergeant Mooney asked.

The young man moaned, shrugged his shoulders, and grudgingly stepped from his car.

"I haven't done anything. I was just sitting here taking a rest. There's no law against that."

"That depends," the police officer replied as he surveyed both the car and the suspect. "What are you doing here?"

"I told you, I was just taking a nap."

"Aw, come on, Larry. You know Libby is living in the Forest Grove Apartments. Were you wanting to see her?"

"It would be nice to see my wife and baby again. No one has the right to split up our family."

"It's been reported to us that you have been following Libby wherever she goes."

"That's not true!" Larry shouted as he slammed his fist into the side of his car. "I've kept my distance from her. I've just been interested in what she's been doing."

Sergeant Mooney took a deep breath. "I must advise you that the state of Montana has very strict antistalking laws. Therefore, you'll have to stay away from this part of Ash Street and make no attempt to see Libby. Otherwise, I'll have to file charges against you."

"That's not fair. I have a right to see them."

"Libby has been advised to see an attorney and obtain a restraining order to keep you away from her and Vanessa."

"And who advised her to do that?" Larry demanded. "I suppose it was that Dutton woman again. She's always meddling in my affairs."

"Whom Libby talks with is no concern of yours. You need to worry about keeping your nose clean while you're on probation. The judge doesn't look kindly on anyone who makes trouble during probation. Now get in your car and go on home. I don't want to receive another report of you being near these apartments."

Larry opened the door, slipped behind the wheel, and intentionally made his tires throw gravel as he sped away. Philip Mooney shook his head with disgust. *Will Larry ever accept responsibility for his behavior and quit blaming others for his problems?*

As Larry cruised the streets of Rocky Bluff, his anger escalated. *I've got to put a stop to that old lady's continual interference with my life. If she's going to interfere with my family, I'll just interfere with hers.*

As he turned onto Main Street, his eyes fell upon a sign in front of a local prominent business. He steered his car into an empty parking space in front of Harkness Hardware Store. Ignoring the expired parking meter, he stormed toward the door forcing other pedestrians to move out of his way.

"Is Bob Harkness here?" Larry demanded of the attractive woman behind the counter.

Nancy Harkness gulped as she recognized the disturbed young man. "He's working in the storeroom if you'd like to go on back."

Not waiting for her to finish her sentence, Larry charged toward the back of the store. Bob was mixing paint in the side room when Larry burst through the swing doors. Larry paused for a moment, not knowing what to say. He wandered aimlessly around and began picking up antique bottles and jars which were on display in the corner. Confusion and rage enveloped him. This seemingly kind family was ruining his life.

Finally, Bob heard the tinkle of glass when Larry replaced a jar onto the shelf. "Well, hello, Larry. It's good to see you. What brings you here today? I was hoping we could get together sometime."

"Yeah, sure," Larry grunted. "My mother told me you wanted to help me. Well, if you want to help me, keep your mother from interfering in my personal life. What my family and I do is none of her business."

"Larry, we are all concerned for you, Libby, and the baby. We just want to have what's best for all of you. Mother has a very soft heart for young people who are hurting."

"Oh garbage. She's just a meddlesome old busybody. I want you to tell her to quit talking to Libby. She's filling her mind full of ridiculous ideas and trying to keep us apart. If she doesn't stop interfering in my life, I'll have to do something drastic."

Bob's face turned ashen as he recalled the painful physical and emotional scars Larry's attack on the high school principal had left on his mother. "Larry, just don't do anything to get yourself in more trouble. You're very upset now. I don't know what has happened, but why don't you sit down and tell me all about it."

"Forget it," he sneered. "Just tell your mother to quit talking with Libby, or else. . . ." With that Larry turned and stomped toward the front and out the door.

Nancy rushed toward her husband. "Do you think he'll try to make good on his threat? I've never seen so much built-up anger in my life."

"Nah," Bob tried to assure her. "He's just blowing off steam. He's all talk. He'll cool off in a little while."

"I sure hope you're right. I don't take threats like that lightly. Are you going to tell your mother that he was here?"

"No, I don't want to worry her and I sure wouldn't want to discourage her from helping Libby. She's doing such a fantastic job with her. I'm sure everything will be okay."

❧

Unaware of Larry's threatening encounter with Bob the day before, Libby joined Edith in her kitchen for coffee and encouragement.

"Have you given any more thought about getting a restraining order to keep Larry away from you?" Edith queried. "I'm sure Stuart Leonard at Legal Services could draw up the paperwork for you. He's a fine young attorney."

"I've been thinking about it a lot since I talked to you yesterday. Soon after I hung up I saw Sergeant Mooney drive up. He was talking to Larry for a while. Larry really appeared angry and was slamming his fist against the side of his car. He then got in his car and sped away. He hasn't been back since."

Edith surveyed Libby's face with concern. She understood how difficult it was for Libby to take a stand against Larry even when her personal safety was in jeopardy. "I wonder how long he'll stay away? A day? A week?"

"As stern as Sergeant Mooney looked I bet he scared him off, but I don't want to take any chances. I'll make an appointment with Legal Services tomorrow."

"That's a good idea," Edith reminded her. "If circumstances change you can always have a restraining order lifted."

Libby sighed. "At least I'm not doing something that can't be undone." She stared out the window at the buds that were beginning to appear on the bare elm tree. The encased buds seemed to give her a ray of hope. Soon new leaves would be springing forth. *I feel like those buds. I want to break out of my shell and make something beautiful of myself like the elm leaves do.*

"Edith, the other day you talked to me about going back to school and getting some training. At the time I didn't think I was smart enough to, but I think I'd like to give it a try. How do I go about it? I'm not sure what I even want to do."

"What are some things you're interested in?" Edith asked as she poured the young woman another cup of coffee.

"Well. . . This may sound kind of strange, but since Larry has been in so much trouble with the law I've been fascinated with the law shows on TV. I even stay up late at night to watch the old Perry Mason reruns. But I know I'd never be able to be a lawyer."

"Have you ever considered becoming a paralegal? Lawyers can't function without them."

"That might have possibilities, but I don't know how I'd ever be able to pay for it."

"They have all kinds of grants and scholarships available for those who attend Rocky Bluff Community College. Teresa keeps abreast on all the different programs available. Why don't we give her a call and ask her to come over?"

"Sure," Libby said with a smile. "Can I use your phone? I have her number memorized by now."

Libby took the phone and dialed the familiar number. There was a long pause as Libby waited impatiently for a response.

"Hello."

"Hello, Teresa. This is Libby. How are you today?"

"I'm doing great and you?"

"Things have really changed since I got my own apartment. Why I called is I'm here at Edith's now and we were wondering if you were free and could come over for a few minutes."

"I'd love to. Just give me a few minutes to freshen up. I'll be there in a half-hour."

Edith and Libby engaged in small talk and playing with Vanessa until Teresa arrived. When Teresa arrived, the three women made small talk over cookies and coffee before coming to the point of the meeting.

"Teresa, Edith said you're familiar with different assistance programs that I might qualify for so that I could attend college."

"Familiarity of assistance programs is part of my responsibilities as head of the Spouse Abuse Center. Career training is an important aspect in helping abused women get on their feet again. Is there a particular field you're interested in?"

"I'm wondering if I'm smart enough to become a paralegal."

"Of course you're smart enough. When you get back in the studying mode, your self-confidence will come back. The main concern is supporting yourself and Vanessa. Social Services has several programs that can help with living expenses and child care. Also, the county bar association provides several grants every year for those interested in paralegal studies. I don't think they've all been claimed for this past school year."

Libby beamed as her thoughts turned inward. *There may be hope for me yet. I might be able to make it on my own without Larry.* "How soon do you think I could start?"

"Right now," Teresa assured her. "Registration for spring quarter is next week. You could begin by taking a lighter load to get back in the swing of things. Then with a couple courses in the summer, by fall you'll be able to lead the pack."

Tears filled Libby's eyes. "Do you really think so?"

"Of course I do," Teresa responded giving Libby a hug as Edith looked on with pleasure.

❧

For the next few days Edith was busy with projects in the church and entertaining her grandchildren after school. However, after four days without hearing from Libby she began to wonder if she had given up on her plans to attend college and was afraid to tell her. Her concerns were removed when her phone rang late Friday afternoon.

"Hello, Edith. This is Libby. I've been meaning to call you for the last few days, but I've been extremely busy."

"I'm glad to hear from you. How are things going?"

"Great. I have all the paperwork filled out for college. I was able to get financial assistance and I register for classes next week. My only problem is I can't find anyone to take care of Vanessa while I go to class. All the daycares are full and no one wants a child for only a few hours a week. You know lots of people in town. Do you know anyone who might be interested?"

Edith thought for a moment. "This may be a long shot and you might not like this idea at all, but I have a young friend who is a teenage mother. She's doing an excellent job with her baby and is trying to get on her feet the same as you are. Would you be interested in meeting her?"

"Sure. If she's nice maybe we can help each other. I qualify for subsidized child care so I'll be able to pay the going rate in the community. How can I get in touch with her?"

"Her name is Beth Slater. I met her via the Crisis Center. I'll give her a call and maybe she could come over Monday afternoon and the two of you could meet."

"That sounds good to me. Call me when you find out if she can come and I'll see if Sonya wouldn't mind driving me over on her way to aerobics class."

❧

Monday afternoon Beth Slater knocked on the door of the Dutton residence. Edith eagerly flung the door open and greeted her with a warm hug as she motioned for her to enter.

"Beth, it's good to see you again. It's been too long since we've gotten together. I hardly recognize little Jeffy."

Beth smiled as she stood her toddler on his feet and removed the coat from his chubby shoulders. "I don't think you've seen him since he began walking. He's become a regular terror on two legs."

"He looks perfectly healthy and happy. I'm so proud of the care you've taken of him."

"The parenting classes you suggested were extremely helpful. Plus, I'm going to get my high school diploma in May. By taking those special classes I was able to catch up with my classmates. I'll graduate a week after my eighteenth birthday. I'm so glad you were on the crisis line the first night I called. I never would have gotten my life together without you."

Edith hung Beth's coat in the hall closet and motioned to follow her to the kitchen. "I have another friend coming over in a few minutes whom I'd like you to meet. She has many of the same challenges you have. Right now she's getting ready to attend the community college."

"Sounds great to me. I've been so busy taking care of Jeffy that I haven't had any time for a social life."

"She is looking for someone to take care of her seven-month-old baby while she attends class. All the daycares are either full or won't take children for only a few hours a week."

Beth raised her eyebrows. "Would it be a paying job?"

"Of course," Edith assured her. "She'll be getting government assistance to help with child care while she goes to classes. She can pay the going rate for day care. Are you interested?"

The young mother beamed. "Sure. This would be my first paying job. I like the idea of being able to pay some of my own expenses. I've had to be on ADC for so long."

"Good. Libby should be here any time. She has a beautiful baby girl named Vanessa. She'll win your heart immediately."

Just then the doorbell rang. Edith moved to the front door as quickly as she could. "Libby, please come in. Beth is anxious to meet you and little Vanessa."

Libby hung her coat in the hall closet as she had so many times before and followed Edith to the kitchen.

"Libby, this is Beth Slater and Jeffy. Beth, I'd like you to meet Libby Reynolds and Vanessa," Edith said as she motioned for Libby to have a chair.

"Hi, Libby. You have an adorable baby."

"Thanks," Libby grinned and turned to inspect Beth's baby. "Jeffy is a real sweetheart with those big brown eyes."

"You wouldn't be any relation to Larry Reynolds, would you?" Beth asked innocently.

Libby flashed a look of embarrassed panic at Edith before she answered. "Yes, he's my husband. . . we're separated right now."

"Oh, I'm sorry. I didn't mean to pry," Beth replied meekly. "I had a friend who said that when she was in junior high Larry was always her hero. He was talented in all sports, good looking, and had a neat sense of humor. She had him up on such a high pedestal that she was devastated when he shot the principal."

"Larry's had many inner struggles. He's such a neat guy and I think I still love him, but I don't dare live with him until he works out his problems. I'm afraid he'll hurt me or Vanessa."

"I hope things work out for you. I know raising a baby by yourself and trying to study is pretty hard."

"Right now I'm trying to find someone to watch Vanessa three mornings a week while I go to class. I'm at the point of no child care, no class."

"I take classes for my high school diploma in the evening and I'd love to take care of Vanessa for you."

The girls began exchanging details of their lives and situations and before the afternoon was over, both were on their way to becoming close friends. Edith sat back and smiled at the mutual support and encouragement they were able to give each other. Mature encouragement was vital in both their circumstances, but the encouragement of a peer in the same circumstances helped to fill a void in both their lives.

five

The crocuses were in full bloom beside the front steps of Edith Dutton's home as Sonya Turner rang the front doorbell. She nervously tightened her scarf against the crisp spring winds.

"Hello, Sonya. Please come in," the former home economics teacher greeted as she thrust open the storm door. "We haven't had a chance to visit since Libby moved into her own apartment."

"Hi, Edith. I'm glad you could see me on such short notice. Your reputation of being the problem-solver of Rocky Bluff is getting around."

Edith chuckled as she hung Sonya's coat in the hall closet. "I'm sure there's others who would describe me differently. Larry Reynolds describes me as a meddlesome old lady."

"I bet someday he'll learn to respect you the way the rest of us do," Sonya assured her.

"Why don't you join me in the kitchen for a cup of coffee? I have a feeling you came over for more than just a casual visit."

Sonya obediently followed her into the bright, airy kitchen. "Yes," she hesitated, "I do need some personal advice. You're pretty good at reading people."

"Comes with experience," Edith chuckled. "Now why don't you tell me about it?" Edith poured the coffee and sat the pot between them.

"Remember Pam Claiborne who was living in the

apartment that Libby moved into?"

"I've never met her, but I've heard a lot of good things about her. Didn't she marry Ed Summer, the new music teacher?"

"Oh, yes. And she's been floating on cloud nine ever since. You'd think she was the only woman who has ever been in love," Sonya giggled.

Edith wrinkled her forehead. "So where is the problem?"

"Pam has just begun selling Beautiful You Cosmetics and she's trying to arrange as many makeup parties as possible. I'd really like to help her, but my apartment is too small and since I'm working all day I don't know many people to invite."

"Now that is one of the easiest problems I've been asked to help solve. I have plenty of space here and I know quite a few young women about your age. Why don't we turn this into a real get-acquainted event?"

"Pam says a makeup party works best if there are between eight and ten guests. I can only think of Libby and Patricia to invite. Can you think of any others?"

"Do you know Beth Slater? She's taking care of Libby's baby while Libby attends classes. And Libby told me about her new friend, Liz, who lives across the hall from her. Maybe she would like to invite her." Edith paused for a moment as she stared out the window. "What about Patricia's sister, Jenny?"

Sonya beamed. "We're now up to seven. There's a lady at work that I know. Her name is Joan. Maybe she would like to come and bring her friend, Kristen, with her."

"Well, that's our guest list," Edith responded. "Now when do you want to have the party?"

"I'll have to clear it with Pam, of course, but how about a week from Wednesday?"

"Sounds good to me. I'll make one of my specialties for dessert."

"I can't let you do that," Sonya protested. "I'll bring the refreshments. It's enough that you provide the place for us to meet."

The two women chatted about Sonya's job and mutual acquaintances for another half-hour and then Sonya hurried to the Spouse Abuse Center where she was scheduled to work for the evening. Edith watched through her picture window as she drove away. *It's so uplifting to have the younger women find their way to my kitchen table. When I retired I was certain I would live in isolation with only friends from the senior citizen's center.*

❧

The days passed swiftly before the scheduled make-up party. The Saturday before the party Edith hired Hilda to clean the house for her. It was going to be fun to have a houseful of young women along with their babies gathered in her home. With a houseful of women coming, however, Roy decided Wednesday night would be a good time to catch up on his paperwork at the Crisis Center.

Promptly at seven o'clock the night of the party, Sonya and Pam arrived at the Dutton residence loaded with boxes and a small suitcase.

"Do you mind if we use your kitchen table?" Pam queried. "It's easier to spread the different products out on the table and it's closer to water."

"Certainly. I guess I'm a little rusty on the requirements of makeup parties." Edith motioned for the pair to follow her to her much-used kitchen table.

While Pam arranged her assortment of products in the

center of the table, Sonya set up extra folding chairs and organized the refreshments. By seven-thirty all the details were prepared for the guests.

Within fifteen minutes eight young women were gathered around Edith's kitchen table. Sonya served lemon bars, mixed nuts, and Hawaiian punch while Pam explained the advantages of Beautiful You Cosmetics. When she completed her presentation, Pam asked for questions.

Libby looked pensive for a few moments and then finally got up enough courage to speak. "All of your pictures and examples only show gorgeous girls. What about those of us that don't have any natural beauty? I can't see spending my money on something like this."

"Libby, you have a lot of natural beauty," Pam assured her. "But you've been so busy being a mother and student that you haven't had the time to develop it. We're all going to have complete facials. We'll experiment with the different techniques and shades of makeup and compare the difference."

"I don't think anything could make a difference on my ugly face, but I'm willing to give it a try," Libby chuckled.

Pam spent the next few minutes going from guest to guest helping them completely remove their old makeup and selecting the most attractive shade for them to try. Little by little Libby's skepticism was replaced by genuine enthusiasm. She learned how to select the right color for different types of lighting. She learned how to blend the blush high on her cheekbones and how to merge three different shades of eye shadow.

"Wow, you look terrific," Jenny observed. "You could get any man you'd want looking like that."

Libby gulped. Her eyes turned distant. "I only want

Larry, but I don't think we'll ever be able to get our marriage together again."

"Time will tell," Edith responded. "The important thing is that you feel good about yourself. Go look in the full-length mirror in my bedroom and see the difference in yourself. Hold your head up and be proud of who you are."

Five minutes later Libby returned to the kitchen with her eyes aglow. "I couldn't believe that was really me in the mirror. The only problem is, my new face makes my clothes look shabby."

The entire group broke into gales of laughter. "I have just the solution for you," Pam said as soon as the laughter subsided. "I've also begun selling a line of women's clothes, Fashions by Rachel. They sent me a lot of samples so that I could begin to spread the word around Montana about their outstanding clothes. If you're not busy in the morning, I'll bring some over to your apartment and see how many fit you. You can be the walking advertisement for Fashions by Rachel at Rocky Bluff Community College."

Libby's face flushed. "I've never been a model before, but it might be fun trying."

The party broke up within an hour with everyone convinced that they were much more attractive than before. Libby could scarcely contain her excitement about the change in her appearance and eagerly awaited Pam's visit.

❧

Early the next morning Pam pulled into her old parking stall at the Forest Grove Apartments. She unloaded the clothing traveler and headed for Libby's apartment. Libby greeted her with even more enthusiasm than she had the night before. Before the morning was over, Libby had learned how to select the right colors and lines for her particular figure. She learned what types of slacks and skirts helped slim her hips and thighs. Best of all, she had an entirely new wardrobe of clothes for only guaranteeing to help Pam introduce Fashions by Rachel around the state.

That afternoon, dressed in her favorite slacks outfit, Libby put Vanessa in a new sweater that Edith had given her and headed for the neighborhood supermarket. As she was pushing the stroller across the parking lot a familiar Maverick pulled up beside her.

"Wow, you're looking great," Larry sneered. "Where did you get those clothes? A new boyfriend buy them?"

Libby's face turned ashen. She looked over her shoulder, but another car was behind her and there was nowhere for her to run. "Larry, you're not supposed to bother me. Did you forget about your restraining order?"

"I didn't look you up. This is merely a chance meeting. Now tell me where you got your new look. Is it some other guy?"

"I'm too busy now to be interested in men." Libby did nothing to hide her disgust. "If you really must know I was over at Edith Dutton's last night and. . . "

Before she could finish her sentence Larry snapped, "I might have known that old biddy was interfering in our lives again. I bet she's trying to get you to look nice so you can find another man. Just you wait. I'll get even with her yet." With that he stomped on the accelerator, left a strip of rubber on the asphalt and sped out of the parking lot. Libby took a deep breath, tried to force a smile on her face, and headed for the front entrance of the store. *I'm glad Larry liked my new look. I only wish he'd waited long enough to hear the real story. When will he ever get over his insane jealousy?*

❧

At 3:22 A.M. the next morning fire sirens pierced the stillness of Rocky Bluff. A red glow lit the business district as flames leaped out the windows of Harkness Hardware Store. Officer Scott Packwood blocked off the street while the firemen hooked up their hoses to the fire hydrant in front of the store. Heavy black smoke poured from the back of the building as the fire consumed the paint inventory. Sharp, piercing explosions followed as the fire ignited the locked case of ammunition. In spite of the hour, a crowd began to gather across the street on the courthouse lawn.

Having secured the area, Officer Packwood called the police dispatch. "Steve, phone Bob Harkness and tell him there is a fire at his store and to come immediately."

"I'll get right on it," Steve responded crisply as he reached for the local phone book.

Within minutes Bob and Nancy were dressed and on their way to the store. Expecting to find a localized fire that was under control they were horrified at the flames and billows of black smoke that were consuming their building. Bob parked his car on the far side of the courthouse square next to a red Maverick. He took his wife's hand and raced across the lawn toward the burning building. He quickly spotted Officer Packwood.

"Scott, what's happened? How'd it start?" Bob gasped. "It looks like we've lost everything."

"I don't think anything could have survived that intense heat. The fire chief is suspicious of arson but they won't be able to begin their investigation until it cools down. Do you have any idea what might have started the fire?"

"No, everything looked normal when we left at seven-thirty. I can't imagine that we have any firebugs in Rocky Bluff."

"Rumor has it that finances were getting kind of tight for you right now," Scott said as his eyes pierced through the darkness toward Bob.

Just then Nancy began to sob hysterically. Bob wrapped his long arms around her and pulled her next to him completely ignoring the policeman's comment. They stood and trembled together as the roof crashed into the building.

"Pretty bad fire, huh?" said a deep voice from behind the couple.

Bob turned and found himself face to face with Larry Reynolds. "The worst I've ever seen in my lifetime," he stammered.

"Might put you out of business, huh?"

"Probably so."

"Have you told your mother that her pride and joy has burned to the ground? I bet she'll really be upset," Larry snarled with contempt. "Could I have the honor of telling her?"

Bob glared at the young man. He was in no humor to deal with a smart-mouthed punk.

As dawn broke over Rocky Bluff, Harkness Hardware lay in ruins. Bob and Nancy waited until the firetruck left and then drove directly to the Dutton residence.

"Bob, Nancy, do come in," Roy greeted as he opened the door wearing his robe and slippers. "Your mother and I were just sitting down to breakfast. Would you like to join us?"

"Thanks for the offer," Nancy replied. "But I'm afraid food would stick in my throat right now."

"Bob, Nancy, is that you?" a female voice shouted from

the kitchen. "Would you like some scrambled eggs?"

"No food for me, Mom. We are bearers of bad news," Bob stammered.

Edith surveyed their tear-stained faces as the couple entered the kitchen. "Sit down and tell me what has happened. You look like you've lost your last friend."

"It's even worse than that," Bob replied as he poured himself a cup of coffee. "We lost the entire store."

"I knew you were having financial problems but it all couldn't have gone up in a puff of smoke overnight. You'll have time to reorganize and liquidate some of your assets."

"Mom, that's exactly what happened. It all went up in a puff of smoke. There was a fire about three-thirty last night and the store is a pile of rubble."

Edith sat in stunned silence as her weakened heart pounded within her chest. "I can hardly believe it. After all the years of hard work George and I put into that store I can't imagine it a pile of rubble. Give Roy and I a few minutes to dress and take us downtown."

Edith and Roy quickly forgot their breakfast and rushed to the bedroom to dress while Nancy and Bob paced nervously around the living room.

As the foursome headed toward the business section of Rocky Bluff, Bob explained the details of the previous night as best he could. "Mom, the strangest part was the number of people that had gathered that time of night to watch the fire. Even Larry Reynolds was there."

"That kid sure gets around," Edith sighed. "Bob, have you contacted your insurance agent yet? I'm sure there'll be a major investigation."

Bob scowled. "I never thought about an investigation. I'll have to wait until ten o'clock until his office opens to call." He hesitated then took a deep breath. "It's hard enough losing everything, I don't think I can fill out a pile of papers. All our records would have been lost in the fire. I don't even know how I can validate my exact inventory."

Bob parked the car in front of the courthouse across from what remained of Harkness Hardware Store. Roy helped Edith from the car and pulled her close to him as she surveyed the rubble. Tears built in her eyes.

"Edith, are you all right?" Roy queried gently. "I don't want this to be too much of a strain on you."

Edith forced a smile. "Of course this is hard, but I know that with Bob and Nancy's skills and the good Lord's help they'll be back in business in a few months. This isn't the end of Harkness Hardware Store, it's a new beginning."

"Mom, I wish I had your faith. You see good during even the worst circumstances." Bob took his wife's hand. "But if everyone will stand behind us with prayer, Nancy and I will do our best to carry on."

six

"Bob, I realize this is a tough time for you and that most of your business records were destroyed in the fire, but we're going to have to reconstruct your assets and liabilities as best we can," Warren Engelwood said as he opened his laptop computer and placed it on Bob and Nancy Harkness's dining room table.

"I'll do my best," the shattered store owner replied as he poured his insurance agent a cup of coffee. "Nancy might be better at remembering the details than I am. She worked with the figures at the end of each day."

"My mind is blank," Nancy stammered. "It quit functioning the night of the fire."

Warren looked at her sympathetically and then turned his attention back to his computer. "First, how much inventory did you lose in each category?" Warren asked as he selected the appropriate data field on his laptop.

Bob sighed, looked over at his wife, and shrugged his shoulders.

"I honestly can't remember. We had a backup tape locked in a metal cabinet in the office, but it wasn't fireproof so I don't know if it survived or not."

"Why don't we go down to the store and see if we can find it?" Warren said as he closed his computer. "If it isn't damaged too badly, I can send it to our central office. They are equipped to restore damaged computer tapes and disks."

"We can take my pickup," Bob volunteered as he

reached for the keys on a hook beside the back door.

Nancy slumped deeper into her chair. "If you don't mind, I think I'll wait until later to see the rubble. Besides, I promised the kids I'd take them down this afternoon."

❧

Solemnly, Bob and Warren climbed over the yellow barricade tape on the side of the building where the office was once located. They moved a burnt beam from the rafters that had lodged against the charred remains of the desk and the metal cabinet.

"Be careful, Bob," Warren reminded his client. "This could be dangerous. We don't know if the floor or walls are weakened enough to collapse. All we want is to get into the file cabinet, then let the demolition crew take over."

"Except for being covered with soot the file cabinet doesn't look in too bad a shape," Bob replied as he forced the key into the lock and turned. "I'm glad I've kept a duplicate key on the same ring as the house and car keys."

Both men held their breath as he shook the key until he felt the lock release. There on the second shelf, seemingly untouched by water or heat, was the backup tape.

"Great," Warren beamed. "It looks like it's still pretty much intact. To save both our time I'll take this back with me. I can do most of my report from the office. Meanwhile, I'll arrange for the crew to come and level the building. They won't be able to begin until the fire inspectors have finished their investigations, but that should be completed within a few days."

The two men climbed into Bob's pickup and headed back to the Harkness home. "Thanks for the ride," Warren said as Bob parked his vehicle in the drive next to the family car. "I'll be getting back to Great Falls and try to get as much done on this today as I can. Good luck."

❧

"Hello, Jean," Edith Dutton greeted as her daughter in Idaho answered her ringing phone. "How are you and Gloria doing?"

"We're doing great. Gloria's a little fussy from teething, but nothing beyond the normal."

"I have some bad news for you," Edith continued. "There was a fire at the store last night."

Jean remained silent for several moments trying to grasp what her mother had said. The store had always stood as an indestructible monument for her. "Did Bob lose much?" she finally queried.

"The store was a total loss. He's meeting with his insurance agent now. I sure hope the insurance will cover enough so that he can rebuild."

"Do they know what caused it yet?"

"The fire inspector is still working on it, but they're suspicious of arson."

"Arson in Rocky Bluff?" Jean shook her head is disbelief. "That doesn't seem possible."

"I know," Edith sighed. "But a lot of strange things have happened here. It's not the sleepy village you grew up in."

"In my time no one would have imagined that a school principal would be shot by a student," Jean said with disgust.

"Not to change the subject, but it sure is nice to have a nurse for a daughter," Edith said, trying to ease the tension.

Jean giggled. "I see it's time for free medical advice coming up."

Edith's voice became serious once again. "You guessed it," she replied as she took a deep breath. "I'm getting concerned about Roy."

"What seems to be his problem?"

"He's tired all the time. It's all he can do to walk from his recliner to the kitchen table."

"Fatigue can accompany a multitude of maladies. Is there anything else?"

"Well, it's all kind of illusive," Edith explained. "He just sits in his chair all day and drinks water. I've never seen anyone consume that much water, even when they were working in the hot sun. On top of that Roy has become extremely moody and that isn't like him at all."

"Without taking a blood test I can't be sure, but the symptoms sound a lot like diabetes. He needs to see a doctor right away to have it checked out."

Edith sighed. "That won't be easy. He's having trouble admitting that anything is wrong. He thinks it's just a sign of advancing age."

"Mom, do your best to convince him that there's a big difference between being old and being sick," Jean begged. "It's imperative that he gets to a doctor right away."

❧

Later that afternoon when Edith confronted Roy with the possibility of diabetes, his reaction was much different from what she expected.

He sat frozen and expressionless for a few moments and then his eyes lit up. "Edith, I should have thought of diabetes before," he said as he took her hand in his. "Maybe I should give Doctor Brewer a call. My mother suffered from it before she died of a heart attack. I'll always remember the final heart attack, but what led up to it faded from my memory. But I do remember her taking shots at least twice a day."

"If you'd like, I'll go ahead and make an appointment for you. You just stay here and rest." Edith leaned over and gave him a hug. Roy had been so good about taking care of her during the long months in which she recuperated from her heart problems, she would do as much as she possibly could in her weakened condition to take care of him.

❧

Two days later, Nancy drove her in-laws to the Professional Medical Clinic. She entertained herself by flipping the pages of *Redbook* and *Better Homes and Gardens.* Thirty minutes later the solemn couple emerged arm-in-arm from the examining room.

"Nancy, they did some lab work and my blood sugar level was nearly 400," Roy began, trying to force a smile. "Doctor Brewer wants to put me in the hospital for a few days to monitor my blood sugar and do further tests to make sure none of my organs have been affected. Would you mind stopping by the house first so I can pick up my robe and slippers?"

"No problem at all," Nancy replied. "Is there anything you need from the store on the way? A new toothbrush or anything?"

"I'm just too tired to get out of the car. But if you wouldn't mind, would you run into the grocery store and get me a soft bristled brush." Roy chuckled weakly. "Toothbrushes they provide in hospitals are like emery boards."

"I'd be glad to." Nancy motioned to a bench just inside the front door. "Why don't you two wait here and I'll go get the car. I had to park at the far end of the lot."

Roy and Edith sank onto the bench and waited for their ride. Neither one wanted to admit the anxiety they were feeling. Edith didn't dare tell Roy that she felt her heart pounding within her chest.

❧

Bob generally relied on his mother to keep him informed about the news of his sister, but now, more than ever, he needed his sister's encouragement in this latest family crisis.

"Hello, stranger," he greeted as he recognized his sister's gentle voice. "How have you been? I'm sorry I haven't checked in with you lately."

"Bob, it's good to hear from you. I understand you're going through some pretty tough times. . .losing the store and everything."

Bob sighed. "That's the understatement of the year. And to make matters worse they admitted Roy to the local hospital this afternoon."

"What's wrong? I hope it's nothing serious."

"His blood sugar was nearly 400. The doctor wants him in the hospital to regulate his insulin and to do further tests to make sure none of his organs are damaged."

"With blood sugar that high it could be serious. How's Mom holding up?"

"You know Mom. She's the strength for everyone. However, when I left the hospital her face was terribly flushed and she looked awfully tired. I tried to get her to go home and rest, but she didn't want to leave until Roy was asleep."

"I think I'd better come," Jean replied without hesitation. "Jim has a few days of personal leave. Now that Gloria's older it won't be difficult to travel with her. We'll leave first thing in the morning."

"I sure would appreciate that," Bob responded. "I'd imagine when Roy gets out of the hospital Mom is going to need some help. I wish you didn't live so far away. You're such an encouragement for everyone."

❧

By seven o'clock the next morning Jean and Jim Thompson locked the front door of their home in Chamberland, Idaho, and fastened their daughter in her car seat. The miles flew by as they cruised the familiar interstate highway and then turned onto a two-lane highway outside of Missoula. They had driven this route many times before, and each time it was different. The freshness of the mountain springtime was all around them.

Twelve hours later the young family pulled into the parking lot of the Rocky Bluff Community Hospital. They checked at the front desk for the room number of Roy Dutton and then hurried down the west wing toward room 116.

As they quietly peeked into the room they saw Roy peacefully sleeping in the bed by the window while Edith was busy knitting in the green chair in the corner.

"Hello, Mother," Jean whispered as she hurried across the room to give her mother a kiss.

Edith looked up with a tired smile. "Hello, Jean. I'm so glad you could come. Bob said you'd be in sometime this evening."

Edith turned to Jim who was holding the baby. "Hi, Jim. How's Gloria? She has grown so much since I last saw her."

"Gloria's doing great," Jim replied as he admired his smiling daughter. "However, I think she's entering her terrible twos early," he chuckled. "When I put her down she can really move."

Jean glanced at her sleeping stepfather. "How's Roy?"

"He's resting comfortably, but it's been quite a struggle. If you wouldn't mind driving me home, I'll fill you in on the details later."

❧

The day after Jean arrived, Roy was dismissed from the hospital. However, before dismissal Edith and Roy received a minitraining session on how to check Roy's blood sugar at home and how to inject his daily insulin shots. Jean had their home spotless upon their arrival. She had spent that morning in the grocery store, in an attempt to restock their refrigerator with foods that were suitable for a diabetic diet. She also knew that same diabetic diet would be healthy for her mother as well.

Jean was not only concerned about her mother and stepdad, but her brother as well. She tried to console him that as soon as the insurance company finished their audit, he could begin to rebuild.

Early the next Monday morning the doorbell rang at the Harkness home. Jay hurried to answer it.

"Hello, is your daddy home?" Warren Engelwood asked as Jay recognized him as the man who came the day after the fire.

"Yeh, just a minute." Jay stepped back and shouted. "Hey, Dad, someone's here to see you."

Bob hurried from the back bedroom where he had been going through hardware catalogs, dreaming of the day he could rebuild.

"Warren, do come in. Can I get you a cup of coffee?"

"I think I'll wait on that." The insurance agent's face was glum. "I'd like you to meet Craig Goosemont. Craig, this is Bob Harkness."

Bob reached out his hand. "It's nice to meet you, Craig.

Won't you sit down?"

The three men sat stiffly on the living room sofa and chair. Warren cleared his throat. "Bob, I have some bad news for you. We were able to reconstruct your backup computer tape. The data showed that your business was in serious financial trouble when the fire occurred. Under those circumstances, combined with the Fire Chief's conclusion that arson was the probable cause of the fire, we have no alternative but to turn our audit over to the county attorney. No insurance claim will be paid until the county attorney's investigation has cleared you of any involvement with the fire. I'm sorry it had to turn out this way."

Bob's face turned ashen. He could not speak for several minutes. His body trembled. "That is absurd. Yes, we were having financial problems, but we were eventually going to get out of it. I'd never think of starting a fire to collect insurance money."

"I'm sorry," Warren repeated. "We have to report our findings to the county attorney. My advice to you is to hire the best attorney in town."

The two men excused themselves and walked briskly from the house. Bob watched from the window as they got into Warren's car and drove away.

"Dad, why did they accuse you of starting the fire? You'd never do anything like that. You're the best dad and the best Christian in town." Jay sobbed as he clutched his father around the waist.

"I don't understand this, son," Bob assured him. "But God has brought us through good times and bad. He won't let us down now when we need Him the most."

Suddenly, Nancy appeared at her husband's side and placed her arm around his broad shoulders. "I don't know how things could get any worse," she muttered through tear-filled eyes. "This is a time when the Harkness clan pools their strength and comes up with a solution. I'm glad Jim and Jean are here now. I think we better have a family meeting before we do anything else."

"I don't want to burden them with my problems when they have enough of their own, but they'll be upset if we don't let them know right away. I'd hate to have them learn from someone else I'm suspected of arson."

Roy was sitting in his recliner watching TV and Edith was resting on the sofa when Bob, Nancy, and the children entered through the back door. Jean was there to greet them.

"Would you like something to eat to start your day out right?" Jean asked lightly.

Bob and Nancy stood in solemn silence.

"Oh, dear. Did I say something wrong?"

"You sure did, Sis," Bob said as he gave her a hug. "Things have gone from terrible to unbelievable. Is Mom busy?"

"She's resting on the sofa. What's this all about?"

"Let's go to the living room and we'll tell everyone our sordid tale of woe."

After retelling the conversation with Warren and Craig, Bob was surprised with how calmly everybody took the news that he was about to be accused of arson.

"Bob, things are going to work out. They don't have any substantial evidence against you. Having a business in financial trouble is not a crime. It happens every day." Edith's voice was calm and steady. "However, I have two suggestions for you. First, go talk with Pastor Rhodes and seek his support and prayers, and then go see Michael Miller. He's the best criminal attorney in town and a good

Christian man. I'm sure he'll be able to get things ironed out for you."

Roy rose from his chair and put his hand on Bob's shoulder. "Bob, you have stood up and confessed when you were wrong regarding the car accident and Pete's death, and God forgave you and saw you through those difficult times. You came out of that a much stronger person. Now when you are falsely accused God will continue to protect you and make you a better person. We're all standing behind you."

Bob relaxed, and the tension lines began to fade from his face. His mother's and Roy's words were a salve to his troubled spirits. With a family like this standing behind him, he could survive anything.

seven

"Gentlemen, I just had an interesting talk with Warren Engelwood and Craig Goosemont, the agents of Bob Harkness's insurance company," Carol Hartson began as Philip Mooney and Scott Packwood made themselves comfortable in the modest office of the county attorney.

"They gave me a copy of an audit they did of Bob's store. It seems that the office safe protected the store's computer backup tape from the fire. The picture the audit shows is not very pretty. Bob was in serious financial trouble. So serious in fact, that as I see it, he only had three options to save his business. He could hit up the bank for another loan, he could go belly up through bankruptcy, or he could torch the place for the insurance. Check with the bank to see if he applied for a loan and if they turned him down. He did not file for bankruptcy and, as we know, the store burned. I want you to go back over your entire investigation step-by-step. The arson inspector for the insurance company believes that Bob Harkness started the fire himself to hide his financial problems."

Phil and Scott looked at each other in shocked disbelief. "That doesn't seem possible," Phil protested. "I've known Bob since he was a kid. He's not an arsonist."

Carol's lips remained tight as her forehead wrinkled. "Phil, I've known Bob all of my life too, but we can't allow our emotions to prevent us from enforcing the law. Go back to the crime scene. There has to be something we have overlooked. Also, this is an election year. We can't let the biggest crime Rocky Bluff has had in years go unsolved."

"We'll do our best," Scott assured her as he and Phil left the room shaking their heads. "We've been through every aspect of this case at least twenty times, but we'll give it another shot."

Phil and Scott strolled briskly across the courthouse lawn toward the burnt-out store. "This is what we get when we have a new county attorney who's out to make a name for herself," Phil sighed. "Ever since she took office she's been no end of grief for the police department. She treats us like we're all totally incompetent."

"It's rumored around town that Stuart Leonard is planning on running against her in the next election. My guess is that if he runs, he'll get it," Scott replied. "He's very well liked because of his work with Legal Services and the representation he provides for the poor."

"He's got my vote," Phil declared. "He's got a good head on his shoulders. He wouldn't be expecting us to waste our time digging through this rubble for the umpteenth time."

"Okay. Let's play her game one more time," Scott declared as the pair walked gingerly through the burnt-out building. "We'll pretend this is our first investigation after the fire."

Phil shrugged his shoulders. "It's obvious the fire started here in the paint room. The fire was much hotter here and even some of the metal shelving melted and the walls are much more charred."

"Paint's pretty flammable. It wouldn't have taken much to ignite it." Scott took several deep breaths as he moved around the building. "There's no odor of gasoline in here."

"Even if there had been gasoline in here by now its

scent would be pretty well gone," Phil replied as he poked the rubble in the back corner. Taking a pencil from his shirt pocket, he leaned over and inserted the pencil into a circular piece of glass.

"What do you have there, Phil?" Scott asked, hurrying toward his friend for closer inspection.

"Looks like the neck of an old glass gallon jug."

"I've never seen one of those before," Scott replied.

"Come on," Phil snickered. "Don't try to tell me that this was before your time. Ma and Pa stores used to sell orange juice in jugs like these. Then along came supermarkets and plastic containers."

Phil placed the piece of glass into a cellophane envelope and handed it to Scott. "Take this over to the lab and see if they can lift any prints from it."

"You're thinking maybe that jug was used as a Molotov cocktail to fire this place?"

Sergeant Mooney shook his head with dismay. "Could be. . .it's possible. We don't have anything else to go on. Get this over to the lab right away. Meantime, I'm off to the bank, then I'll bring in Bob Harkness for questioning."

❧

Edith tried hard not to let the latest family crisis upset her. She knew she would have to find something more to occupy her time and thoughts. The crisis line had been fairly inactive during the pleasant summer months. Libby Reynolds was busy taking classes at Rocky Bluff Community College while Beth Slater watched little Vanessa and her own baby, Jeffy. The warmth and fellowship of the makeup party remained with her. Little by little plans began to materialize in her mind. Wednesday afternoon she gave her pastor a call at his church study.

"Pastor Rhodes," she began after sharing a few moments of small talk. "If you have some free time sometime this week would you mind stopping by for a cup of coffee? I have an idea for a church project I'd like to talk to you about."

"Sounds good to me. How does tomorrow at two o'clock sound to you?"

"Great, the coffee pot will be ready."

Edith hung up the phone and scratched a few notes to herself. She wanted to have her plan well thought out before she presented it to anyone else. An undertaking like this had never before been attempted in Rocky Bluff.

"Roy, how have you been?" Pastor Rhodes queried as he shook the older man's hand.

Roy beamed. He was always glad for a visit from his pastor. He had been with him through good times and bad. "I'm doing a lot better," Roy assured him. "I've really been trying to take care of myself. I take my insulin faithfully and Jean prepared a pretty rigid diet for me to follow before she went back to Idaho."

"I'm glad to hear that," Pastor Rhodes gave a playful glance toward Edith. "I'm certain your wife is keeping you in line."

"You better believe it. All sweets are barred from the house and a lock has been placed on the refrigerator door."

After Edith served coffee and placed a vegetable tray in front of them on the coffee table, Pastor Rhodes looked over at Edith. "What kind of project do you have in mind for the church? I'm always interested in ways to expand our ministry."

"I know you've been aware of my activities with some of the young mothers in the community." Edith's eyes sparkled with enthusiasm. "I'd like to help start a group for young mothers who have little training and little support from family members. I envision a multigenerational group that would help fill the parenting gap. We could call it MEM—Mothers Encouraging Moms."

Pastor Rhodes remained silent a few moments as he stared out the picture window. *That's a fantastic idea. Why hadn't I thought of that years ago?*

He then turned his attention back to Edith. "I like that. Tell me more while I take some notes. I don't want to miss a thing."

"I thought each session could feature a topic presentation, perhaps a local authority. There could also be a craft time, musical entertainment, devotions, and 'ice-breaking' games," Edith explained.

"It sounds like you've really thought this through. How do you propose we start?"

"I was thinking that we could form an executive committee. Maybe Beth and Libby would like to help us," Edith paused and cleared her throat before continuing. "Perhaps a couple of ladies from the Ladies Aid could also serve on the executive committee. They could have a wealth of ideas of things to try."

"Edith, since you seem to have a pretty good handle on this, why don't we set up a meeting date, call the group together and officially lay the groundwork? The church calendar is pretty open this summer, so you could pick any time you'd like."

"How about a week from Wednesday?" Edith queried. "That would give me time to get a few women together to brainstorm. I'll host the get-together. Could you be able to join us then, Pastor?"

"I wouldn't miss it for the world. I'll try to compile a list of local human resources you might consider for speakers."

After Pastor Rhodes left the Dutton home, Edith immediately set about calling potential executive committee members. She knew she had to keep her mind busy so she would not think about the loss of the store and her son's uncertain future.

❧

"Rick, I appreciate you taking the time to visit with me," Sergeant Mooney said as he entered the plush office of the president of First National Bank in Rocky Bluff. "I'll try to keep this as brief as possible."

"This sounds serious," the middle-aged banker replied as he motioned for his guest to be seated. "What can I do to help?"

"I understand the Harkness Hardware Store had an account in your bank."

"They've been customers of ours since George Harkness originally opened the store."

"Could you tell me a little about its financial condition before the fire?"

"Of course I don't know about his other liabilities, but I do know that a few weeks before the fire Bob Harkness filed an application for a loan with us so he could pay some of his vendors. I guess they were pressing him pretty hard."

"Did you give him the loan?"

"That was one of the hardest things I've had to do as a banker," Rick confided. "I hate denying a loan to a longtime friend, but the recession has hit the local farmers so hard that they're not buying anything from anyone right now. They're just making do with what they have. Our loan committee felt a loan to Bob at this time was too great a risk for us to take."

"Do you have any ideas how he was going to meet his financial obligations?" Philip asked. The possibility of a solid Rocky Bluff citizen being an arsonist sent chills through his body.

Rick shook his head sadly. "I haven't a clue. But with the figures he put on his loan application, he was going to have to do something fairly soon."

Phil thanked the banker for his help and shuffled through the lobby into the brightness of the summer afternoon. *I wish I wasn't the one responsible for this investigation. I'm just too close to the family to be objective. I've participated in a multitude of church and community activities with the Harkness family. Bob just couldn't have started the fire.*

He trudged back to the police station and slumped into his chair. He took the manila folder from his "Active" file and shuffled through a few pages. Finding what he was looking for, he copied a telephone number to a piece of scratch paper and dialed the phone.

"Mr. Warren Engelwood, please. This is Sergeant Mooney of the Rocky Bluff Police Department calling."

"Just a moment, I'll buzz him," a pleasant voice replied.

Within a few seconds a male voice came on the line. "This is Warren Engelwood. May I help you?"

"Yes. This is Phil Mooney and I'm investigating the Harkness Hardware Store fire. I understand that the store was insured by your company."

"That's right," Warren replied. "We hired a special arson investigator and the circumstances do not look at all good for the owner of the store. In fact, we had a long conversation with your local county attorney. She's quite a go-getter."

Phil shook his head with dismay. "That she is. What's the company's opinion of the case?"

"First of all, Bob had a strong motive to collect fire insurance. According to his records that we were able to salvage from his computer backup tape, he was on the verge of bankruptcy." Warren was unable to hide his disgust for small town law enforcement. "Being the owner of the store he obviously had all kinds of opportunity to start the fire, plus he had the means to do it."

"That's all circumstantial," Philip reminded him. "Do you have anything concrete?"

"I gave everything we have to your county attorney. How she uses it is up to her."

Unable to get any satisfaction from the insurance agent, Phil ended the conversation and took his pocket tape recorder from his desk and added a new cassette. The only thing left to do was interview Bob Harkness.

Sergeant Mooney again picked up the telephone and dialed the familiar number of Bob Harkness's home.

Bob answered the telephone on the first ring. "Hello, Phil. What a pleasant surprise. What can I do for you today?"

"I'm sorry, but this is not a personal call. I'm going to have to ask you to come down to the station. We need to question you further about the fire. I'll spare you and your family the embarrassment of coming to your house to pick you up."

"I'll be glad to do anything I can to help, but I think I've told you everything I can about the fire. I just wish I knew how it started."

"Please come down right away. I'll be in my office."

"Thanks for the courtesy, Phil. I'm on my way."

When Bob arrived at the police station Phil directed

him to a small conference room in the back and started his tape recorder. "Bob, I understand you were having some financial problems at the store shortly before the fire."

"I'll have to admit I was," Bob mumbled. "I was considering bankruptcy, but I knew that would kill Mother. She and Dad had worked so hard to build up the business."

"So what were you planning to do?"

"I had hoped to get a loan from the bank, but they turned me down."

"Was the store well insured?"

"That is the only good thing about this entire situation. Mom and Dad took out an excellent policy when they first opened and I've kept it up through the years." Suddenly he stopped and stared at the police officer. Disbelief enveloped him. "Phil, you don't honestly think I started the fire in order to collect the insurance?"

"The circumstances don't look very good for you right now."

Bob glared at the officer. "You've got to be kidding. We've known each other for years. You know I could never do anything like that."

"Our personal relationship has nothing to do with this. We have look to look at the facts and right now the facts don't look very good for you. Bob, whenever police anywhere investigate a crime they seek the answers to three questions. Who had the motive to commit the crime, who had the opportunity to commit the crime, and what means were used to commit the crime. You definitely had a motive to torch your store and plenty of opportunity. As of right now, we don't know how it was done—the means. But you fit the answers to two of those three questions."

Bob clutched his fist under the table as he tried to maintain control. "This is absolutely preposterous. I don't want to answer any more questions until I have a lawyer present."

"That's a very wise decision," Phil assured him. "You're free to go now, but we'll be in touch. Until this is solved, you are not to leave town."

Bob Harkness left the conference room not knowing whether to cry or to fly into a rage. He felt as if his world had just crumbled around him. Everything he had ever stood for had been called into question.

On the way down the hall Bob passed Scott Packwood. "How's it going, Bob?" Scott asked and was surprised when Bob didn't respond.

With a shrug of his shoulders, Scott entered Phil's office where Phil sat dejectedly.

"Phil, good news!" Scott almost shouted. "You were right. We hit pay dirt. There were prints on that bottleneck. You'll never guess whose."

"All right, I'll bite—whose?"

"Larry Reynolds."

eight

Bob stepped into the brilliant Montana sun. *What right do the birds have to sing and the sun to shine?* he pouted as he walked toward his car. *This entire thing is absurd. Mother will be heartsick to think they're seriously considering pressing arson charges against me. I have to find a gentle way to break the news to her.*

Bob blindly drove across town and parked his Ford Taurus in his driveway. He burst through the back door, slamming it behind him.

"Bob, what happened?" Nancy asked as she stopped the motor on the vacuum cleaner.

"The police actually think I started the fire for the insurance money. Their entire case is based on the store's financial problems."

"That can't be." Nancy was adamant as she put her arms around her husband. "We've known most of those policemen all our lives. They're our friends. How can they possibly think that?"

"That's what I said, but Phil told me that our personal relationship has nothing to do with this. They have to look at the facts."

"But what facts?" Nancy protested. "They don't have any."

"It's all circumstantial." Bob headed for the refrigerator and took out a pitcher of tea. "Otherwise, they would have arrested me on the spot. They even told me not to leave town until this is over. Would you like to have a glass of iced tea with me?"

"I need something to help me cool off," Nancy replied as she pushed her dark hair back from her face and slumped into a chair at the kitchen table.

Bob handed a glass to his wife and then took a big sip from his own. "I'm the one that has to cool off. I don't think I've ever been this angry in my life. I know right always triumphs in the end, but it sure looks bleak now. I'm going to have to break the news to Mom and Roy and that's not going to be easy."

"We've gotten so used to being concerned about her health, but now we also have to be concerned about his. They say stress is one of the most dangerous agitators of diabetes."

"Mother always taught me about inner strength and peace with God. I often wondered how she did it," Bob admitted. "Now I'm the one who's going to have to ignore my feelings and fall back on what she taught."

Bob took several deep breaths followed by another swallow of iced tea. "I think I can handle talking about this without being angry. Let's go over and see them before they hear it from someone else."

Roy and Edith Dutton were resting in their recliners in the living room when Bob and Nancy arrived. Bob tapped on the door, opened it, and exclaimed, "Don't get up. We'll let ourselves in."

Edith released her footrest and sat upright. "Do come in. It's good to see you both. I was wondering how you were doing."

Bob gulped. He had to choose his words carefully. "We're doing fine. We just wanted to stop over and check on you." Bob studied his stepfather relaxing in his chair. "How have you been doing today, Roy?"

"To be honest, this isn't one of my better days," he confided. "I feel extremely nervous and irritable. Sometimes, I wonder how Edith puts up with me."

Edith smiled as she reached out and took his hand. "I'm beginning to understand the symptoms. I generally know when it's really the disease complaining or you."

"Bob, I hope you realize what a jewel of a mother you have. She's always putting everyone else's needs before her own."

"It took me many years to see it, but she's definitely head and shoulders above the rest of us." Bob paused and studied his mother's graying hair and smooth complexion. Her peaceful serenity glowed through her wrinkled face. "I did have a minor setback today. Philip Mooney called and asked me to come down to the police station. It seems they are seriously investigating me for arson."

Roy looked puzzled. "But why? They couldn't possibly have any evidence against you."

"I know," Bob sighed, "but because of my financial problems they assumed I had a motive and, of course, I would have had all kinds of opportunity. All they're looking for is how I supposedly started the fire. I'm going to have to see my attorney tomorrow to find a way out of this."

"Any good lawyer will be able to clear your name," Edith assured him. "I don't think you'll have anything to worry about. It's all part of the process until they find the cause of the fire."

Bob nodded in agreement. "But it sure makes it difficult being accused of something as absurd as that. God has seen me through some other pretty tough times, I'm sure He'll see me through this as well."

❧

Philip Mooney stared at his partner. Embarrassment and shame enveloped him. "Scott, I've just done the most absolute stupid thing in my entire career. I caved in to the influence of our novice county attorney and believed that Bob was guilty of starting that fire. I came as close to arresting him as I possibly could without actually doing it. I feel like such a fool."

Finally, Phil cleared his throat and gazed at his partner with intensity. "Now tell me more about the prints on that bottleneck."

"There are prints on the glass and they definitely belong to Larry Reynolds."

"How did the lab make the identification so quickly?"

"They decided to compare them against our local bad boys' prints on file before sending them to the FBI. Larry's were the sixth set they compared and they got a match."

"Funny," mused Phil. "I had never even thought of Larry for this one, but remember all the talk he's been doing about getting even with the Harkness family? That kid really hates those people. Blames them for all of his troubles, but yet if Edith hadn't stopped him when she did, he would have killed Grady Walker and be doing life today instead of probation."

"Yeah," agreed Scott. "He's one weird dude. Shall we bring him in?"

"Yes, go over to the city magistrate's office and get a warrant for his arrest then meet me back here. I've got some paperwork to do. We'll head out to his parents' ranch soon as I finish it."

"That's one reason I'm glad I'm only a patrolman—no paperwork," Scott teased as he left Phil's office.

❧

That afternoon Nancy and Bob rented a video and went to the Dutton home just to try to get their minds off their problems. When the movie was over, Edith gazed at the tension-filled face of her son. She longed to help take the burden away. "It's a beautiful day. Why don't you and Nancy go play a round of golf and get your minds off all this? Take Nancy out to the steakhouse afterwards. Stay out as long as you like. Roy and I will stay with the kids."

"We can't impose on you like that," Nancy protested weakly.

"It's no imposition. We can rest just as well at your house as at our own," Roy grinned. "When it's mealtime we'll just call Pizza Palace for home delivery."

Bob studied his mother's tired face. "Mom, I appreciate this. You're a real jewel. I'll bring the car around to the front so you won't have to walk so far."

❧

As Phil and Scott drove to the Reynolds's ranch, each felt a deep sense of relief. Finally, the case would be closed and they would have Carol Hartson off their backs. As the patrol car entered the lane to the ranch, they spotted Ryan playing in the yard with his dog.

"Pretty fancy tricks you have your dog doing," Scott shouted as he got out of his car.

"I've taught Ralph a lot of new stuff," Ryan responded proudly. "I don't think Larry taught him a thing when he had him."

"Speaking of your brother, is he home now?" Phil asked.

"Yeah. He's in watching TV. He's been a real couch potato since he moved back home. What do you want him for?"

Phil gulped. It was obvious that Ryan thought the world

of his brother, in spite of his mocked sarcasm. "We just want to talk to him for a few minutes."

Ryan turned his attention back to Ralph while the officers stepped onto the wooden porch of the old ranch house. Mrs. Reynolds answered the door dressed in a flannel shirt and blue jeans. The lines on her face tightened.

"May I help you?"

"We would like to talk with Larry. Is he home?"

"Yes. He's in the living room. Won't you come in?"

Larry rose from the sofa as the two officers entered the room. "What do you want?"

"We have a warrant for your arrest, Larry. The charge is arson for starting the Harkness Hardware Store fire."

"I don't know anything about it. All I know is that they got what they had coming."

Frances Reynolds scowled at her son. "Be quiet, Larry. You're in enough trouble as it is."

"I was just a bystander," Larry sneered. "It sure was fun watching that building burn."

Scott didn't say a word as he took Larry by the arm and led him to the patrol car. The three men rode back to town in silence. They led the young suspect back to the same conference room Phil had used a few hours earlier with Bob Harkness. They closed the door behind them.

Philip cleared his throat. "Larry Reynolds, you're under arrest for the arson fire of the Harkness Hardware Store. You have the right to remain silent. You have the right to have an attorney present during all questioning. If you cannot afford an attorney, one will be appointed for you. Anything you say can and will be used against you in a court of law. Do you understand these rights?"

"Of course. I've heard 'em all before," Larry snarled. " I didn't start that fire, so I don't need a lawyer."

Phil and Scott had perfected their interrogation techniques after years of working together. They had the "Good Cop-Bad Cop" routine down to a science. Phil, the more experienced of the two, was always the "Bad Cop."

They had also devised a technique of their own they called "Knock 'em-Sock 'em." They would seat the suspect in a chair positioned in the middle of the room. Phil would stand to the suspect's right while Scott stood to his left. First Phil, then Scott would bombard the suspect with questions scarcely giving him time to answer. They would keep this up for hours until the suspect either told them what they wanted to know or until they were convinced the suspect was innocent.

Phil decided to employ "Knock 'em-Sock 'em" in their interrogation of Larry. Scott positioned the chair and directed Larry to sit. Larry, ever contemptuous of authority, moved the chair a few inches before sitting.

"Okay," he stated in his most arrogant and cynical voice. "I'm ready whenever you are."

Phil scowled at the suspect. "Why did you set fire to the Harkness Store?"

"I didn't."

Then it was Scott's turn. "We know you did."

"No, you don't," Larry countered.

Phil stared at him sternly for several moments before he spoke. "You tossed a glass jug filled with gasoline through the store's rear window and then followed that up with a lighted match."

Larry sighed with disgust. "I did no such thing."

Gradually Larry became less cocky as his self-confidence was continually challenged. Phil would ask him a question, he would turn his head toward Phil to answer, and then Scott would throw a question at him. When he turned toward Scott to answer, Phil would query him. It was all extremely unnerving and Larry hoped it would end and soon.

"Why do you hate the Harkness family?" Phil snarled.

"Everybody knows how much trouble they've. . . ." Larry suddenly realized what he was saying was self-incriminating and he let his voice trail off.

Scott could not let this opportunity pass. "You admit you hate them then?"

Larry looked at the floor. "Yes. . .err. . . no, I don't . . . ."

"You've told everybody in Rocky Bluff who'd listen how much you hate them," Phil reminded him.

"That was just talk." Larry was blubbering now, on the verge of crying.

"We can put fifty witnesses on the stand who will testify you swore to them you would get even with the Harkness family," Scott retorted, unmoved by Larry's whimpering tone.

"I. . .I was just running off at the mouth."

"Tell us how you torched the place, Larry. It'll go easier for you," Phil explained sternly.

Larry's voice began to break. "You got nothing on. . . ."

"Oh, yes we have," Scott assured him. "You got away with the attempted murder of Grady Walker because your smart lawyer pleaded your youth and temporary insanity, but this time we have the goods on you."

Larry began to panic. "No, you haven't!" he screamed.

Phil's eyes seemed to pierce the suspect's soul. "You're an adult now, Larry, and you told too many people that you would get even with the Harkness family to plead temporary insanity this time."

Larry started sobbing. "I didn't do it."

Scott looked at his partner. "Shall I show him, Phil?"

"Go ahead. It will cut down on his excuses."

Scott held up the cellophane envelope containing the bottleneck. "Remember this, Larry? It's the neck of the glass jug you filled with gasoline and then threw through the rear window of the store."

Larry was now utterly confused. "I didn't do it. I never saw that thing before."

"If you never saw it before then how come your fingerprints are all over it?" Phil challenged.

Larry was totally dumbfounded and couldn't speak. He tried to choke back his sobs.

"We found it in the paint room where the fire started," Scott stated firmly.

Larry's face whitened. His hands and shoulders began to tremble. *These guys are for real. I could go to the state pen in Deer Lodge for something I didn't do. I was able to plead temporary insanity as a minor when I shot Mr. Walker, but nobody will defend me now.*

Vanessa's innocent face flashed before him. *I can't let my little girl grow up knowing her daddy's in jail. Libby's done such a good job taking care of her while I was never there to help. Now there's a court order keeping me from seeing them. And it was all caused by my own stupidity.*

Larry pictured Libby's sweet face and long blond hair on their wedding day. He pictured her the day he saw her in the supermarket parking lot with her new hairdo, makeup, and clothes. *How can I possibly throw away such a thing of beauty? And to think I would actually beat up on her for the dumbest reasons.*

Finally, Larry, shaken and more afraid than he had ever been in his life, was able to respond. "I don't doubt that you found my prints in that room. I was there with Bob

Harkness less than two weeks ago. Ask Bob, he'll tell you so himself."

Phil shook his head in disbelief. He had heard so many excuses throughout his law enforcement career that this was just another one to add to his list. "Larry, you're entitled to one telephone call before I take you to your cell. You can make it now. I suggest that you call an attorney."

"I want to talk with Bob Harkness. He has always offered to help me, but I've been the one who's been obnoxious toward him."

"Come on," Philip retorted. "You don't think Bob Harkness is going to get you out of this mess. Remember, you've been telling everyone around town you were going to get even with him and his mother. Now you've been arrested for taking away their years of hard work. I know they're good people, but they are not going to come to your defense. You'll now finally have to pay for the consequences of your own behavior."

"I know it would take an act of God for anyone to come to my rescue in such circumstances. But I have nowhere else to turn. Please let me try," Larry pleaded as tears streamed down his cheeks. Every fiber in his being cried for help and there was only this faint ray of hope. *If God and the Harkness family will help me now, I'll make a whole new shift in my life. I'll get a steady job, I'll quit drinking, I'll be the best husband and father out there.*

Larry looked nervously around the bare room. The two police officers stared at him. A dismal cell waited for him just a few yards away. *Dear God, I've been such a fool. Please help me. Show me what to do. Please forgive me and help others forgive me too, especially Libby.*

Scott stood up and went to the next room. He returned

in a few moments with a telephone and Bob Harkness's phone number written on a scrap of paper.

Larry hurriedly dialed the number.

"Hello," a mature voice greeted.

"Hello, is Bob Harkness there?"

"I'm sorry. He and his wife are out for the remainder of the day. This is Bob's mother. May I take a message?"

nine

"Hello, Mrs. Dutton, this is Larry Reynolds. I need to talk with Bob right away," Larry stammered into the phone.

"I'm sorry, but Bob won't be home until late tonight. Is there something I can help you with?"

Larry hesitated. *Is this offer coming from the same person I wanted revenge against ?* he wondered. "You mean after all I've done you'd be willing to help me?" he said with disbelief.

"Of course I'll help you, Larry," Edith replied. "I'd like to see you have a productive life. Yes, you've made your share of mistakes, but you have a lot of potential. Your parents have given you a good foundation, and you have a lovely wife and child. I remember the days when you were on the honor roll and were a class leader as well as a star athlete."

Tears welled in Larry's eyes. "The good times seem like another lifetime ago."

"But your life isn't over," Edith explained. "It is never too late to turn yourself around."

"I'm beginning to doubt that," the young man whispered. "If things don't change in a hurry, I'm looking at spending the next ten years of my life sitting in the state pen in Deer Lodge."

"Why is that? You're out on probation. There's a restraining order keeping you from bothering Libby, but that isn't enough to send you to Deer Lodge."

"Those are the least of my worries," Larry explained. "I've been arrested for starting the fire at the hardware store. I'm in jail until I can prove I didn't do it."

Edith visualized the panicking young man on the other end of the line. "Larry, Bob won't be back until late tonight, but I'll have him come to the jail first thing in the morning to see what he can do to straighten out this mess."

"Thanks, Mrs. Dutton," Larry sighed. "You won't be sorry you helped me this time. I'm really sorry for telling everyone that I was going to get even with you for messing up my life. If you hadn't intervened, I might have killed Mr. Walker and anyone else who was in my way. If you hadn't intervened, I might have seriously injured Libby and Vanessa. I promise you'll never regret this. Someday you'll be able to be proud of me again."

Edith hung up the phone, returned to the living room, and sunk into her recliner. *Whatever happened to the simple, happy days of Rocky Bluff? Life is becoming too complex and stressful for our young people. I wanted my grandchildren to enjoy the same peaceful community and state that I did, but I fear those days are gone forever.*

❧

By nine o'clock the next morning Bob walked into the police station. Sergeant Philip Mooney was working the front desk. He looked up and smiled. "Good morning, Bob. What brings you out so early in the morning?"

"Mother got a strange phone call from Larry Reynolds late yesterday. What's going on?"

"We've arrested him for arson. We now have evidence that he started the fire at the hardware store," Philip explained.

Bob could scarcely conceal his annoyance. "But early yesterday you were almost ready to charge me with starting the fire. What's changed?"

"When we went back to the store we found the neck of an old glass jug with Larry's fingerprints all over it. It's the perfect shape for a Molotov cocktail."

"Can I see the piece or is it confidential?" Bob queried.

"I don't see a problem with you looking at it," Philip replied. "Just a moment and I'll get it from the safe."

As the police officer laid the clear cellophane envelope on the counter, Bob burst out laughing. "That's the top of an old orange juice jug that my dad used to cool his drinking water. Dad kept it full of water in an old ice box. I haven't used it in years and it was on a shelf with a bunch of old jars and bottles in the paint room."

"But how would Larry's fingerprints have gotten on it if it was in the back of the store?"

"About a week before the fire, Larry stopped at the store to talk to me. He was pretty steamed about my mother's influence in getting a restraining order to keep him from bothering Libby. He marched right to the back room where I was mixing paint. I did notice him handling the bottles. I imagine he'd never seen any like those before."

"Well, I guess you just shot down the only substantial evidence we have against him. I'll have to have the charges dropped against him. Would you like to come back with me while I tell him?"

"Sure." Bob followed the police officer down the long corridor to Larry's cell. The clang of the doors behind him sent shivers through his body. *So that is the most feared sound to any prisoner. That ought to be enough to scare anyone straight.*

"Larry," Sergeant Mooney began as he unlocked the cell. "You have a visitor. You were right. Your faith in God and the Harkness family has paid off. Bob told me you were in the paint room visiting with him about a week before the fire. I understand you were pretty interested in his antique bottle collection."

"Yeah, I'd never seen anything like them before. I got so interested in them that I almost forgot what I'd come to see Bob about," Larry replied. "I think I picked up nearly every bottle on the shelf before he turned around."

"Since Bob came and collaborated your story, I'll let you go home now. Just don't leave town until this is settled," Sergeant Mooney said as he motioned for him to leave.

Larry did not waste any time leaving the cell. As he walked down the narrow corridor he turned to Bob. "Thanks. I really appreciate this. I don't know how I can ever repay you."

Bob put his hand on Larry's shoulder. "Why don't you come home with me for a little coffee and conversation and then I'll drive you back to the ranch?"

"I'd like that. I'm really serious about getting my act together. I can hardly believe that after all I've done, you and your mother are willing to help me."

For the next two hours Larry and Bob visited around their kitchen table. The topics ranged from everything from stress management, anger control, and problems with the law to the fire and their individual families. As time passed Larry kept eyeing the phone on the wall. "Would you mind if I used your phone? I'd like to give Libby a call."

"You know you have a restraining order not to contact her in any way," Bob reminded him. "How about I call her and explain the circumstances, and then ask her if she'd like to talk to you?"

"Sounds good. At least that way she wouldn't get scared

and hang up before I had a chance to explain what I have to say."

Bob reached for the phone. "Do you know her number?"

"I've had it memorized since the day she got her apartment. It's 789-2345. It's easy to remember."

Bob dialed the number and waited. One ring. . .two rings. . .three rings.

"Hello."

"Hello, Libby, this is Bob Harkness. How have you been doing lately?"

"I'm doing great. I'm really busy with school and taking care of Vanessa."

"Why I'm calling concerns Larry. I suppose you've heard they arrested him for starting the fire at the hardware store."

"I heard that before class today," Libby replied. "I know he doesn't have a great track record, but I can't believe he actually did it."

"You're right, he didn't do it," Bob assured her. "His fingerprints were found on the neck of a glass jug in the paint room. I went to the police station this morning and explained that Larry had been there just a week before the fire and he was handling the jars then. They released him and their investigation is continuing. He's with me now."

Libby broke into a broad smile. It felt as if a weight were lifted from her shoulders. "I just knew it couldn't be true. In spite of everything, I've always believed in his innate goodness."

"Libby, we know there is a restraining order that keeps him from calling you, but he's sitting right here and would like to talk with you."

"Please put him on. I want to hear directly from him

what is going on."

Bob handed the phone to Larry. "Hi, Libby. Thanks for talking to me. I've done a lot of stupid things in my life. Most of the time I never got caught. This time I could've got sent to Deer Lodge for something I didn't do. If it hadn't been for the Harkness family coming to my aid I'm sure they would've convicted me."

Libby's heart began to soften as she listened to that familiar voice. "When I heard that you'd been arrested I just couldn't believe you did it."

"I'm really serious about getting my act together this time," Larry tried to assure her. "I know you've heard that from me a lot. Every time I hit you I promised you that I'd never do it again, but I always did. I'm truly sorry for the hurt I've caused you. Someday I hope you'll be able to forgive me."

"Larry, I forgave you a long time ago. But there's more involved here than simple forgiveness. I have to be certain that you have changed. I can't risk you hurting me or Vanessa the next time you become angry."

"I understand what you are saying, but would you be willing to start over fresh? Not from the night they took you to the battered spouses home but from the night we first met."

"Are you saying you want to start dating all over again?"

"Exactly," Larry replied with confidence. "We'll take it slow and easy and not repeat the same mistakes. Maybe we can begin by starting to go to church together."

Libby's eyes filled with tears. "I think I'd like that. But I don't want to feel any pressure. There are a lot of hurts that need to be healed."

"Thanks, Libby. Of course, first we have to get the restraining order lifted. Then after that we can start dating again."

"I'll see what I can do," Libby promised with tears running down her cheeks. "It was good talking to you. Goodbye. We'll be in touch."

Larry breathed a sigh of relief as he hung up the phone. He turned his attention back to Bob. "Thanks for letting me use your phone. Would you mind giving me a ride back to the ranch now? I have a lot of fences to mend with my family."

❧

That afternoon Philip Mooney and Scott Packwood were summoned to a meeting with Carol Hartson, the county attorney.

"Well, guys," Carol began. "Let's review where we are so far." She took out a manila folder and began to refer to some handwritten notes. "We know Bob Harkness was in dire financial straits and pulling every string he could to stay in business. He applied for a bank loan but was turned down. His creditors were pressuring him to pay up. That's sure motive aplenty to fire the place for the insurance. As the owner, Bob had access to the store any time. So much for opportunity. But thus far, we haven't been able to ascertain the means. How the fire was started. Bob is smart enough to fire his place without leaving any clues. But I've known Bob Harkness all of my life and I can't believe he would do anything like that."

She paused for a few moments, chewing on the end of her pencil. "Then we have Larry Reynolds. He hates the Harkness family and holds them personally responsible for all of his troubles. He has vowed revenge to everyone who will listen. That's motive. And let's not forget his fingerprints were found in the paint room, Bob's explanation notwithstanding. That points to opportunity. I've also known Larry Reynolds all of my life and I wouldn't put anything past him. But I don't believe Larry is smart enough to start a fire without leaving some telltale signs behind."

Carol surveyed the two police officers slumped in their chairs before her. She could not let this case go unsolved. After all, this was an election year. The local newspaper was calling her constantly for an explanation. "Well, gentlemen, does this mean we are stumped?"

The two uniformed officers looked at one another and then at Carol. Both nodded their heads in the affirmative.

"Is it time to call in the experts?"

Again Phil and Scott nodded their agreement.

Carol pressed the push to talk button on her intercom: "Lily, get me Bruce Devlin at the State Crime Lab in Missoula, please."

Carol held the phone loosely to her ear and turned her attention back to the officers. "Kind of hard on the old ego to have to admit we can't solve this one without help, isn't it?"

Phil shrugged his shoulders in disgust. "This is the first time in my career as a police officer that I've been unable to complete an investigation."

Lily's voice came over the intercom. "Miss Hartson, Mr. Devlin is on line one."

"Thank you, Lily." Carol put the phone tightly against her ear and pressed the flashing light on the phone base before her. "Hello, Bruce. How is the luck of the Irish these days?"

"Carol, you don't need luck if you're Irish. Just being Irish is enough. What can I do for you?"

"We have a situation here that cries of arson. Two viable suspects, each with strong motives and ample opportunity. But we can't put our finger on the how. May I borrow Marty Sanchez for a day or two?"

"Well, Marty's in Kalispell right now on another case, but I can probably shake him free by Friday. But you'll have to pay his transportation. I'm over budget now."

"Friday will be fine. Go ahead and send him down round-trip air and my office will reimburse yours."

"Right, I'll get back to you on flight numbers and times Have a good day, Carol."

"You, too, Bruce, and thanks."

Carol hung up the phone and turned back to the officers. "As soon as Bruce gives me Marty's arrival time, I'll let you know. Thanks for coming in."

Once the two officers were out of Carol Hartson's office, Scott turned to Phil. "Who is Marty Sanchez?"

"Just the best arson investigator in the western United States and Canada. Quite possibly the best of all in both countries," Phil replied. "He started out working for an insurance company, but as his fame grew so did the demand for his services. He's been in the business over twenty-five years. The past ten with the State Crime Lab."

"Do you think he can put his finger on our case?" Scott queried. "We've been over it from every possible angle."

"I'd stake my reputation on it. Marty Sanchez is one of the most respected arson investigators in the country. He's probably investigated more torchings than anyone in the field. Whenever cops in the West have a burn they can't make out they call on Marty. Beats me, though, how a greenhorn like Carol heard about him."

"I'll bet she called some old-timer somewhere and asked his advice," Scott retorted. "I bet it really hurt her pride to have to ask someone for help."

Phil laughed. "You're probably right, Scott. Few people

outside of law enforcement ever heard of Marty."

"In other words," summarized Scott, "if Marty Sanchez says its arson. . ."

"It's arson." Phil finished Scott's sentence for him and then added, "Let's get back to headquarters. I wouldn't want the chief to hear about Marty Sanchez coming in from anybody but us. Word travels in Rocky Bluff faster than our feet can get us across the street."

"Boy, that's for sure," agreed Scott. "Rumors are generally a lot more interesting than the facts."

ten

Libby paced around her living room. This was almost too good to be true. *I have always said I believed in miracles and that people can change. But could it happen to Larry? He has claimed he was going to change so many times before, how can I know that this time is different?*

She picked up Vanessa and cuddled her against her breast. *Wouldn't it be better if Vanessa were raised in a two-parent family instead of only having one? Why do the innocent have to suffer from the stupid actions of adults?*

Realizing that she needed another adult to talk with, she picked up the phone and called a familiar number.

Edith Dutton answered on the fourth ring of her phone. "Hello?"

"Hello, Edith. This is Libby. How are you doing today?"

"I'm doing great. How are you and Vanessa?"

"We're fine. In fact, I think we're on the verge of a real breakthrough, but I'm just not sure," Libby explained, scarcely able to contain her excitement.

"Larry and I just had the first seemingly honest conversation in our lives."

"But I thought there was a restraining order prohibiting him from contacting you." Edith could no longer contain her puzzlement. The last she had heard from anyone was when Larry called the night before from the jail asking for Bob.

"Bob was able to have him released. Bob called me from his home and asked if I wanted to talk to Larry. Of course, I had to say yes. My curiosity was getting the better of me. When Larry started talking, I couldn't believe what I was hearing. He always apologized every time he beat me, but it never really sounded sincere. This time he sounded like he really meant it. He wants to start our relationship all over again. In essence, he wants us to start dating again. I'm excited and scared at the same time."

"I imagine you would be having a lot of mixed feelings. This afternoon the executive committee of MEM is meeting here at my house. Why don't you plan to stay for dinner afterwards and we can have a long talk about this?"

Libby smiled. "Thanks for the offer. I really need to talk to someone."

"I'm always here to listen," Edith replied. "That's the least I can do."

"You know the new MEM group has meant so much to me. Just meeting with others who have also gone through the same frustrations of raising children has really been an encouragement to me," Libby explained. "I'd like to do more to help others who've gone through some of the same problems I've had."

"I'm sure you'd be good at that," Edith replied. "You've learned a lot about yourself, the meaning of love, and marriage these last few months. In fact, I was talking with Teresa the other day and she was commenting that they were needing more volunteers at the Spouse Abuse Center. Why don't you give her a call?"

"Do you really think I'm ready?"

"With God's help you can do anything," Edith assured her. "Teresa will provide you with the training each step of the way."

The two women chatted a few minutes about the latest antics of Vanessa and then hung up. They both felt they were on the edge of something great, but they had to be sure.

❧

At nine-fifteen Friday morning, Philip Mooney and Scott Packwood waited impatiently for the Treasure State Airline flight from Missoula. Julio Raphael Martinez-Sanchez was the last to deplane from the twin-propeller eighteen-seater, affectionately called a "Flying Cigar." Although his wife called him "Julie," no one else would dare. A third generation Montanan, he was proud to be an American, but yet equally as proud of his Mexican ancestry. Marty was dressed in a plaid western shirt and blue jeans. When traveling out of state, he always wore a three-piece business suit, but when he was home in Montana he dressed for comfort.

Scott watched the graying expert approach as he clutched a manila file folder tightly in his hands. He thought about what Phil had told him about Marty. *If anyone could figure out how the fire started, it would be Marty Sanchez. Marty had twenty-five years' experience as an arson investigator and was well respected by all the police forces in the western United States and Canada. When Marty says its arson, it's arson.*

"Welcome to Rocky Bluff," Philip said as he extended his hand to the investigator. "How was your flight?"

Marty burst into uproarious laughter. "Remember I came in a 'Flying Cigar,' he responded with glee. "It was similar to the roller coaster rides I enjoyed as a kid."

"They do have that reputation," Scott agreed. "Yet, we're thankful Treasure State flies into the small towns. Otherwise, we wouldn't have any air service at all and we'd have to drive one hundred and fifty miles to Great Falls to catch a flight."

"Only those who really want to get here will fly those things," Marty chuckled. "That way Montana is preserved for only the adventuresome at heart."

"By staying semiisolated we protect Montana as the Last Best-Kept Secret of the Country," Philip said as the three men headed toward the waiting patrol car.

"By the way," Scott interjected as he handed the manila folder to Marty, "we brought the file on the Harkness fire along with us. I thought maybe you'd like to review it on the way to the site. It definitely has me stumped."

"Thanks, I appreciate that," the arson expert replied as he opened the back door of the patrol car.

The three men rode in silence as Marty perused the material. Every word was filed in his long-term memory bank for future reference. Upon arriving in the business district, Philip parked the car in front of the courthouse and the trio walked across the street to the burnt-out remains of Harkness Hardware. Not waiting for an explanation, Marty started right to work.

After a few minutes of watching Marty work in absolute silence, Scott whispered to Phil. "He doesn't talk much, does he?"

"No, but he doesn't miss much either," Phil whispered back.

Marty repeatedly returned to the paint room. Phil, Scott, and the local fire investigators had all concluded the fire had started there. But how?

With a pencil firmly gripped at the eraser between the

thumb and forefinger of his right hand, Marty stirred through the rubble. Pausing at an electrical outlet in the northeast corner of the paint room, using his pencil, Marty pulled up the remains of the electrical wiring for a closer look. He took out a small pocket knife and scraped the wiring free of debris.

Phil and Scott watched in amazement while Marty concentrated on the outlet itself. He examined it thoroughly. Using the blade of his pocket knife, he scraped through debris to the metal of the two screws in the outlet. Finally he stood and took a long look at the only window in the room now devoid of panes. He then looked at the only door leading from the paint room to the main part of the store.

The two police officers remained silent while the arson investigator wandered around the room, poking here and there with his pencil. Evidently, he found what he was looking for as he held up the remains of a tin can, smelled it, tossed it aside, and then picked up several more just like it.

Tossing the last can aside, Marty left the paint room and went to the rear of the building. He stopped at the window and peered through it into the paint room. He then directed his attention to the ground as if looking for something. Finding what he was looking for, he poked it with his pencil.

Phil could no longer contain his curiosity and silently went over to see what Marty was so interested in. To his surprise it was pieces of glass. *Why would he be so interested in the glass?* Phil wondered. *There is broken glass all over the place.*

Marty then walked back to the rear of the building and stood by the window. He removed a carpenter's tape measure from his pants pocket and handed one end to Phil.

"Phil, hold this for me."

The police officer dutifully obeyed. Marty measured the distance from the window to the glass. He placed the tape measure back in his pocket and returned to the paint room. He then went directly to the electrical outlet in the northeast corner and again picked up the burned and frayed electrical wiring.

Phil and Scott could scarcely contain their suspense when Marty finally spoke. "This is a paint room — here the store owner mixed the paint the customer wanted. His paint is stored here along with his paint thinner. Paint thinner is a highly flammable liquid and it also gives off noxious fumes. The ventilation in this room consists of only one window and only one door. That should be enough if both of them were kept open, but according to the Fire Chief's report, they were both kept closed. The door was kept closed to prevent the paint odors from entering the main part of the store and the window was always closed for security purposes."

Holding up the electrical wiring for Phil and Scott to see, Marty continued. "See this electrical wiring? It's copper." He then held up the electrical outlet. "See these two screws in the outlet? The copper wires are wrapped around these screws that are then tightened to hold the wires in place. These screws are aluminum. Copper and aluminum are incompatible in electrical fixtures. When electrical current is passed through them they vibrate. But copper and aluminum vibrate at different speeds. This vibration causes friction. Friction generates heat. The heat then became so intense it caused this union of copper and aluminum to spark."

Marty cleared his throat and wiped the sweat from his brow with his red checkered handkerchief before he continued. "In this enclosed room with all of its paint thinner fumes, the sparks ignited the fumes and we had a tremendous explosion. So tremendous that pieces of glass from this window were blown twenty-seven feet from the rear of the building. With the window gone, oxygen was sucked into the room and everything went up in flames."

Phil and Scott look at each other in amazement. He had it all figured out in thirty minutes while they had been working for weeks on this case. Finally Phil spoke, "You mean it's not arson?"

"No way. Given the ingredients of paint, paint thinner fumes, no ventilation, incompatible electrical wiring, you have a catastrophe just waiting to happen," Marty replied with confidence. "Say, can one of you drive me back to the airport? I'd like to catch the next 'Flying Cigar' back to Missoula. My grandson's playing in his first Little League game tonight and I promised him I wouldn't miss an inning. Tell your county attorney I'll mail her my written report in a few days."

❧

That afternoon, Scott and Philip returned to Carol Hartson's office. Carol surveyed their confident stride and smiles as they entered the room. "You look like you have some answers," she observed. "So whom do I prosecute? Bob or Larry?"

"Neither one," Philip replied with a scowl. "It was not arson. The fire was caused by old, incompatible wiring in a room filled with highly flammable fumes."

"To me it's a relief that we don't have to prosecute a community leader or a scared kid," Scott interjected, unable to hide his disdain for the county attorney's eagerness to have a high-profile case. "Would you like to contact the *Herald* or should we?"

Carol slumped in her chair. "I'll call them. They called me this morning while I was in court and I was supposed to return their call. I was waiting for your report before I phoned so I better get on it. It'll probably make the lead story for the Sunday edition," she sighed.

The two officers left her office shaking their heads in dismay. "I'm even more convinced than ever to see Stuart Leonard in that position. Let's go talk to him tonight about getting his campaign organized. We'll volunteer our wives as campaign managers."

Scott look at Phil with amusement. "You mean you can get by with volunteering your wife without first asking her?"

"Of course not," he snickered, "but it's fun thinking about it. Now let's go finish our paperwork. This case is closed."

As soon as the two officers returned to their headquarters, Phil briefed his chief on the case and received his permission to notify the two former suspects that they were off the hook. Scott called Larry at his parents' ranch and relayed the good news to a very relieved young man.

Phil called Bob Harkness, who was equally relieved that the ordeal was over. Phil explained to Bob that the county attorney would notify the *Rocky Bluff Herald*, but that he wanted Bob to hear it from the police before he read about it in the paper.

Bob was absolutely dumbfounded that such a devastating fire could have been caused by something so simple as incompatible electrical wiring. He resolved then and there that his new store would have state-of-the-art electrical fixtures and plenty of ventilation.

❧

Three days later the phone rang in the Robert Harkness home. Nancy sighed as she headed toward the phone. "I wonder who that could be. The phone seems to be ringing off the hook these last few days."

"Hello, Mrs. Harkness?" a cheerful voice greeted.

"Yes it is," she replied politely. "May I help you?"

"Is Bob home? This is Warren Engelwood in Great Falls."

Nancy took a deep breath. The last few times he had called had only brought disappointment and accusations. "He's in the basement. Just a moment and I'll get him."

Nancy walked to the top of the stairs. "Bob," she shouted. "Warren Engelwood is on the phone. Something must be wrong. He almost sounds cheery this time."

Bob hurried up the steps three at a time. "Hello," he panted into the phone.

"Hello Bob, this is Warren. I finally have some good news for you. I just received the arson investigator's report from the crime lab in Missoula. We are ready to settle your insurance claim for the full amount. We'll have the check in the mail first thing Monday morning so you can go ahead and level the building and begin reconstruction. Good luck with your new store!"

Bob's face began to glow. He could hardly keep from shouting but he controlled himself and calmly replied, "Thank you. Thank you very much. I really appreciate you getting this settled so soon."

Bob hung up the phone, picked up his wife, and whirled her around the kitchen. "Bob, what is it?" she gasped as the air was nearly pressed out of her lungs by Bob's excitement.

"They just received the arson investigator's report and

we're going to be reimbursed for the total value of the store. We can begin rebuilding immediately."

"Praise the Lord," Nancy shouted and then in a calmer note added, "It's been tough, but I never doubted that God wouldn't see us through this."

eleven

"Mother, great news," Bob shouted as he stuck his head through the Duttons' back door.

Edith straightened her reclining chair. "Bob, come on in. Is the rest of your family with you?"

"Of course," he replied as Jay and Dawn hurried past their father to give their grandmother a hug.

Nancy could scarcely contain her excitement. "We stopped to get you and Roy and treat you to dinner at the steakhouse."

"I'm always ready for a juicy steak," Roy grinned. "What's the occasion?"

Bob stretched out on the sofa, extended his long legs, and placed both hands behind his head. "I just got a call from Warren Engelwood. They just received the report from the crime lab and they're going to mail me a check for full replacement value. We're back in business again."

Edith beamed. Instinctively, she walked across the room and gave her son a hug. "I'm so happy for you. I knew everything would work out in the end."

"I'm sure glad I listened to you and Dad and kept full coverage on the store. You don't know how much I was tempted to cut back on coverage when the premiums were due and the cash flow limited," Bob admitted.

"I learned a long time ago to expect the unexpected," Edith replied as she sat next to her son. "I've lived through floods, droughts, hail, and even shootings. I didn't see any reason why we'd eventually escape fires as well. I just didn't expect one of this magnitude."

"Edith, why don't you hurry and freshen up?" Roy chided. "I can almost taste my steak already."

Minutes later the family was gathered around a large, circular table in the center of the dining room at Beefy's Steakhouse. Dawn's eyes bounced around the room, awed with her acceptance in an adult environment. Jay was able to mask his excitement. After all, he was almost thirteen and needed to appear cool and very mature.

"Pick the best on the menu," Bob encouraged lightheartedly. "Tonight we celebrate. Monday we start work and won't have time for anything more than hamburgers."

"So how do you plan to attack the rebuilding of Harkness Hardware?" Roy asked as he closed his menu with decisiveness.

"Labor costs are what's going to kill me," Bob replied. "So I want to do most of the work myself. I think my old pickup is going to make lots of trips to the landfill."

"You won't be able to do all the cleanup yourself," Edith insisted. "It takes at least two strong backs to move the heavy stuff."

Roy leaned back in his chair and took a sip of his water. "I've been thinking about that. Good help is hard to find, especially here in Rocky Bluff. Everyone who wants a job already has one."

"This may be a long shot," Edith replied hesitantly. "But what about Larry Reynolds? He's applied for several jobs around town but everyone's afraid to hire him because of his police record."

"Hmmm. I never thought about that," Bob paused a moment and stroked his chin. "I can't afford to pay him much, but maybe if I offer the spare room in the basement he'll be a little more interested. Working long hours like we'll be doing for a while, I can't expect him to make that long trip from the ranch every day."

Just then the waitress appeared to take their orders. Building plans were postponed until Monday. Tonight was a time to enjoy each other and good food.

Dawn was anxious to tell about the events of the first week of school while Jay was excited about having made the middle school's flag football team.

"I'm glad they changed to flag football this year," Nancy said as she took another bite of her chocolate mousse dessert. "There were getting to be too many injuries during the middle school's tackle football games. Last year alone there were a dozen boys on the injured list. I was to the point of not letting Jay play football this season if it was going to be that rough."

"The decision to switch from tackle to flag football in the middle school was a long time in the making. Traditions die hard in Rocky Bluff," Edith recalled. "Even when I was still teaching there were all kinds of studies showing the permanent damage done to growing bodies when they were forced to produce before they were developed enough to do so. I'm glad the kids can now learn the fundamentals of football without risking major injury."

Roy turned to the young man sitting beside him. "Jay, I want to be at your first game. When is it?"

"Right after school next Friday. I was hoping that you and Grandma could come. You never missed any of my Little League games."

"We wouldn't miss it for the world."

The celebration evening ended much too soon. Everyone knew it would be constant hard work until the store was back in operation, but the Harkness/Dutton family was a family that thrived on challenges.

❧

One night while Libby was studying for her class on bankruptcy forms her mind kept drifting back to Larry's phone call. She closed her book and stared out the window into the blackness. It was now time to take action. She picked up the phone and dialed the Donald Reynolds home. Ryan answered the phone and promptly shouted, "Larry, it's for you. Sounds like Libby."

"Hello," Libby said as her estranged husband answered the phone.

"Hello, Libby, how have you and Vanessa been doing?" Larry asked.

"I'm fine," the young mother replied. "However, Vanessa is having another bout with an ear infection. The doctor says that if it persists she'll have to have tubes put in her ears."

"I didn't know she was having trouble with her ears." Larry's voice portrayed his genuine guilt. "I'm not much of a father when I don't know when my own child is sick, am I?"

"There was no way you could have known. After all, there is still a restraining order in place which keeps you from contacting us."

"Libby, would you consider having that order lifted? I'd really like to spend time with you and Vanessa, but I don't want to do anything to jeopardize my probation. I had an awfully close call of going to jail for a long time and I don't want to have even a minor offense held against me. Would you like to have the restraining order lifted?"

Libby took a deep breath. This was a time she had been hoping and praying for, but was she ready? Could she trust being with Larry again? Yet, the softness and concern in his voice softened her doubts. "I'd like that. It is more difficult than I expected being a single parent of a baby. There are so many decisions to make as to her care that I'd like to share."

"Then if it's okay with you, I'll go down to Legal Services tomorrow. Maybe Stuart Leonard will be able to convince the judge to have the restraining order lifted. I heard he is thinking about running for county attorney, but perhaps he'll have time for another case."

"If it would help, I'd be willing to testify that I'm no longer afraid of you and that Vanessa needs to get to know her daddy."

A lump built in Larry's throat. "Thanks, Libby, I can't tell you how much this means to me. It's one thing to say you forgive me, but it's something else for you to believe in me enough to put aside your own fears and doubts and act like I'd never hurt you."

"Larry, I've always seen the gentle side of you and have known your potential, but it was your temper that always seemed to get the better of you."

"I know," the young man mumbled, "but from now on I'm going to think first before I shoot off my big mouth and make stupid mistakes. The consequences just aren't worth it."

"Larry, as soon as the restraining order is lifted, I'd love to see you again. You won't believe how much Vanessa has grown," Libby said. Suddenly a cry came from Libby's bedroom. "Sorry, I have to run. It sounds like she's waking up from her nap. Motherhood beckons."

"'Bye, Lib. I'll be in touch."

❧

Saturday morning Larry paced restlessly around his parents' ranch home. He would go from one minor project to another. TV had long since lost its appeal to him, especially Saturday morning TV. He ignored the distant ringing phone and his younger brother's muffled response. Suddenly there was a loud and clear shout, "Larry, telephone."

Larry hurried to the phone. "Hello?"

"Hello, Larry, this is Bob Harkness."

After a few moments of small talk Bob got to the point of his call. "Larry, I just received word that the insurance company is going to provide complete replacement value for the store, so I'm ready to rebuild. However, I'm going to need another set of strong muscles to help clean up that mess. Would you be interested?"

Larry stood motionless. He had never been offered a job before. Until now he had to try to support himself and family by doing handy-man jobs on demand. No one trusted him with anything more than a lawn mower or snow blower and an occasional hammer or paintbrush. "Yeah, sure, Bob. When would you like me to start?"

"Eight o'clock Monday morning sound okay to you?"

"I'll be there."

"Larry, I want to warn you up front that I won't be able to pay anyone more than minimum wage until the store is in operation again. We'll be working from sunup to sunset for as long as we can. Time is getting short and we need to get as much done as possible before the snow flies."

"I understand. I'm just anxious to get back to work. Life has seemed so pointless since I moved back to the ranch."

"I can imagine," Bob agreed. "I've been getting plenty bored myself waiting for the insurance company to come to a decision." He paused a few moments before continuing. "Larry, I have a spare bedroom in the basement. If it would be more convenient for you, you can use it until you get your feet on the ground again."

Larry could hardly contain himself. "I'd love to. In the evenings I'd like to begin spending time with Libby and Vanessa, and it would be great if I didn't have the long drive to the ranch every night."

"But what about your restraining order?" Bob queried. "I don't want you to do anything to put your probation in jeopardy."

"Oh, I'm getting that taken care of," Larry assured him. "Stuart Leonard is petitioning the court to lift the order. He's pretty sure it will go through because Libby said she'd testify that she is no longer afraid of me and that it would be in Vanessa's best interest that I take a more active parenting role."

"That's great," Bob replied. "If you need another character witness, I'll be willing to testify to the change you have made and that you now have steady employment."

"Thanks for the offer. I need all the help I can get." Larry gazed out the kitchen window. The leaves on the trees in the yard and the field beyond reflected brilliant orange, yellow, and red. Never before had the colors seemed so vivid. "If it's all right with you, what if I bring my toothbrush in about eight o'clock Sunday night? Then I'd be ready for a bright and early start Monday morning."

"Sounds good. We'll leave the light on in the basement for you."

❧

The first week of work sped by for Bob and Larry. The cleanup was tiresome and dirty. After numerous trips to the landfill at the end of each day, they both hurried home and showered, ate a huge dinner that Nancy had prepared, and dropped into bed. Mutual understanding and respect came with each backbreaking hour.

At two o'clock Friday afternoon Bob looked at his watch. "How time flies when you're having fun," he chuckled. "I almost forgot that Jay's flag football game is at three-thirty. I promised him I'd be there and bring Mom and Roy. Doesn't your brother Ryan play on that same team?"

"That's all he could talk about since school started."

"How about coming with us? We can always squeeze another person into the car."

"Do you think people will accept me back? I haven't set foot in that school since I was unceremoniously led out by the police after I shot Mr. Walker."

"You've paid for that. No one holds that against you anymore," Bob assured him. "Your presence will be a testimony to the entire community that you've changed."

"Well, I've always wanted to see Ryan play. I'm sure Mom and Dad will be there too."

❧

Two hours later Bob, Nancy and Dawn Harkness, along with Roy and Edith Dutton and Larry Reynolds huddled together on the wooden bleachers of Rocky Bluff Middle School's football field. Gaiety was in the air as the crisp fall air whisked about them.

"Larry, isn't that your mom and dad coming in now?" Edith asked as she pointed to a middle-aged couple at the far right of the bleachers.

"It sure is," Larry replied as he waved to his parents.

"Why don't I go down and ask them to join us?" Bob said as he stood and began climbing across the bleachers.

The Reynoldses beamed at the invitation of socializing

with another family of their son's teammate, but even more, the chance to watch their older son enjoy the friendship of those he'd considered his enemies just a few weeks before was overwhelming. Maybe there was hope for him yet.

Ryan and Jay both carried the ball several yards while their families stood to cheer them onward. During the second quarter, everyone was on their feet with excitement when Ryan made a forty-yard touchdown.

During the halftime, Larry and his father decided to go to the refreshment stand. After they received their hot dogs and soft drinks they turned to return to the bleachers. As they rounded the corner they were face to face with Grady Walker. Larry froze in his tracks. This was a moment that he had dreaded ever since he shot Grady, but he knew that someday he would have to face it. *What to say? What to do?*

"Hello, Mr. Walker," he said cautiously. "I'm glad to see you again."

"Hello, Larry. How have you been doing lately?"

"I've been doing great these last few weeks." Larry paused and cleared his throat. "Mr. Walker, there is something I've been wanting to say to you for a long time. I'm truly sorry for all the pain and suffering I've caused you. I know there's nothing I can do to make it up to you. I just want to beg your forgiveness, although I know I don't deserve it."

Mr. Walker shook Larry's right hand vigorously while he clasped Larry's shoulder with his left. "Thank you, Larry. I forgave you many years ago. However, there is one way you can make things up to me. Have a full, rich, productive life."

"Thank you so much," Larry stammered. "I won't

disappoint you this time."

❧

It was a large and happy throng that exited the Little Big Horn County Courthouse in Rocky Bluff, Montana, that Tuesday morning. Larry and Libby Reynolds led the procession followed by Roy and Edith Dutton, Bob and Nancy Harkness, Grady Walker, Donald and Frances Reynolds, along with Sergeant Philip Mooney and Officer Scott Packwood of the Rocky Bluff Police Department in full dress blues, minus side arms. Along with them, lest we forget the man who orchestrated it all, was Legal Services Attorney Stuart Leonard.

Thanks to Stuart's excellent presentation and expert examination of the witnesses who volunteered to testify on Larry's behalf, Judge Milton Eubanks lifted the restraining order he had imposed on Larry to prevent him from seeing or otherwise annoying Libby and Vanessa. They were now legally free to start their lives over again.

Stuart called Libby first and she told the judge that in the past few weeks Larry had changed and was again the man she knew and loved. Edith Dutton related that she had always known that Larry was innately good and needed love and patience more than he needed punishment.

Grady Walker followed Edith. He had a two-and-three-quarter-inch scar that ran along his left temple and over which no hair would grow. The scar was put there by the bullet fired by Larry Reynolds. Grady testified that the Larry Reynolds who had begged him for forgiveness at the flag football game was the same Larry Reynolds he had known as an outstanding student and athlete at Rocky Bluff High. That was typical of Grady. He would carry the scar and the memory of that shooting to his grave, but in his heart he had only forgiveness.

Bob Harkness pleaded with the judge to show Larry the same compassion Roy Dutton had shown him after his son's death in an auto accident for which he, Bob, was responsible.

Phil and Scott were not there as friends of Larry Reynolds. They were there because they were proud members of one of the most outstanding law enforcement communities in the nation. Montana's peace officers had a code of ethics they had forged over a hundred years of bringing rustlers, claim jumpers, horse thieves, bank robbers, murderers, and highwaymen to justice. They would fight just as hard to free an innocent man as they would to convict a guilty one. Larry's response to their "Rock 'em -Sock' 'em" interrogation was what they had come to expect from an innocent man. They would testify on Larry's behalf, not because they were friends of his, which they were not, but because they had seen a change in him they believed to be sincere and as Montana peace officers their code would permit them to do no less.

There were hugs, handshakes, tears, and backslapping all around. The tears mostly came from Larry, who thanked his God for blessing him with friends and neighbors like these.

twelve

Kim Packwood and Jessica Mooney had never taken an active role in the political process but this year they were shaken out of their complacency. Law enforcement had become a second love for them and they felt it imperative to elect an experienced lawyer to the position of county attorney. To their way of thinking, Stuart Leonard had the most integrity and was the most intelligent, compassionate lawyer in the county. One crisp fall afternoon they drove to the Rocky Bluff Legal Services Office.

"Hello, ladies, may I help you?" The receptionist behind the desk greeted the pair as they stepped into an unadorned office.

"Hi, Pat," Kim responded. "It's good to see you again. Is Stu busy? We have a proposition we'd like to discuss with him."

"Just a moment and I'll buzz him," Pat replied as she lifted the receiver and pushed the red intercom button.

"Yes," a deep voice answered.

"Kim Packwood and Jessica Mooney are here to see you."

"Send them right in."

Before the pair could reach the office door Stu emerged to greet them. "Do come in," he said as he held the door open for them. "Make yourselves comfortable. Can I get you a cup of coffee?"

"Thank you, I'd appreciate that," Jessica replied.

Kim nodded in agreement. "Thanks. I'll have one as well."

After exchanging a few moments of social pleasantries, Jessica got right to the point. "Stuart, the entire community appreciates the work you're doing at Legal Services. You've been a friend to the poor for many years. You're an excellent lawyer and you're well respected in the community."

Stuart's face flushed. "Well, thank you. I appreciate your confidence. However, I have a feeling I'm being flattered for a reason."

Kim chuckled. "I guess you can see right through us. We do have ulterior motives."

Jessica studied his dark inset eyes. "Stu, we were wondering if you would run for county attorney," she continued. "You know how many problems we've had with the present county attorney. Carol just doesn't have the experience to handle the pressure. Maybe in five or ten years she'll be ready, but not now."

Stu stroked his chin. "Hmm," was all he said as he sat silently gazing at the bright orange elm tree outside his office window.

The two women sat uncomfortably waiting for him to answer. *Are we being too presumptuous in trying to get someone to run for political office? After all, we have no experience in politics ourselves.*

"The thought has crossed my mind. In fact, my wife and I were just discussing the possibility the other night," Stuart finally admitted. "However, I'd hate to give up my work at Legal Services. Here I feel like I'm making a major contribution to the unfortunate people in our county, but there are times when I do feel restless and ready for a change."

"You would make an even greater contribution in the county attorney's office," Kim replied. "If you choose to run, Jessica and I are willing to work for your campaign."

Stuart chuckled. "How can I turn down an offer like that? Two comanagers right at my doorstep."

"We could also recruit some students of the paralegal department at the community college to help with your campaign," Jessica explained. "For many, this will be the first election that they will be able to vote in and a good time for them to get involved."

"Okay," Stu replied. "With support like this, I guess I can't say no. I'll go over to the county clerk's office tomorrow and file the necessary paperwork as candidate for county attorney. I'll be in touch with you in a few days so we can hold a planning meeting by next Saturday. Maybe you could even have a few recruits from the college attend."

The two women grinned, thanked him profusely, and shook his hand as they left his office. Excitement was in the air.

❧

At the next meeting of MEM, Edith gave a half-hour presentation on long-range goal setting. Then they broke into small groups to discuss their individual goals. Beth and Libby ended up in the same group.

"I'm having trouble making long-range goals," Libby admitted. "It seems all I can focus on is how I can survive my next exam."

The others in the group snickered sympathetically. "We've all been in that position," Bea Short said. "You at least have a midrange goal to finish your paralegal course. Otherwise, you wouldn't be working so hard."

Libby smiled. "I guess you're right. I'm really looking forward to getting my diploma in December. Last year at this time I never would have dreamed that I could even get into college."

"Libby, I don't think I've ever told you this before," Beth Slater began. "But you've been a real inspiration to me. I've watched you go to college and make good grades while still taking care of Vanessa. I'm beginning to wonder if I could do the same myself."

Edith Dutton, who had been rotating from group to group, joined their group in time to hear the longing in Beth's voice. "Of course you can go back to college, Beth. Nothing is impossible with God's help."

"Yeah, Beth, if I can do it, you can do it," Libby chimed in. "Fall quarter is over in December and winter quarter begins the first of January. Why don't you start then?"

Beth hesitated as all eyes were focused on her. "Maybe I will," she said thoughtfully. "When I was a little girl I always imagined myself as a secretary, but I'm having to go to night school to get my high school diploma.

"Several people in my class did the same thing," Libby assured her. "They went back to school and got their high school diploma, then they were accepted into the community college. I'll go with you to the student services center tomorrow and they can help you get registered."

Beth beamed as everyone in the small group, both the young moms and the older women, encouraged her to go for it. A deep sense of satisfaction enveloped Edith. Her primary goal of the group was being met—mutual encouragement across generational lines.

❧

"Before we start class today, I have a few announcements to make," Libby's instructor in her bankruptcy forms class began after the students had made their way noisily into the room. "One of the advantages of attending the community college is that you are close to the political process. Regardless of what your particular political persuasion may be, I urge each of you to get involved in the local elections coming up this fall. One such opportunity is the organizational meeting of the "Stuart Leonard for County Attorney" committee this coming Saturday morning. It will be at ten o'clock in the meeting room of the Downtowner Hotel."

Libby's ears perked up. *I've got to go to that,* she told herself. *Stuart was so good to Larry and me when he took Larry's case to have the restraining order lifted. Maybe I should call Larry and tell him about Stuart running for county attorney.*

Libby's attention focused back on the instructor in front of the room. "And now, class, please take out today's assignment and pass it forward."

❧

At nine-thirty that night, Libby phoned the Bob Harkness residence. "Hello, Nancy," she greeted as a friendly voice answered the phone. "This is Libby Reynolds. I hope I'm not calling too late."

"No, of course not," Nancy assured her. "I was just finishing loading the dishwasher. With the men working until the last ray of sunlight is gone we have been having some pretty late dinners."

"Does Larry happen to be handy?" Libby asked.

"He just went to the basement. Just a moment and I'll

call him."

As soon as Larry heard that Libby was on the phone he came bounding up the stairs and rushed to the phone. "Hi, Libby, how are you?"

"I'm fine," she assured him. "I'm sorry I called so late, but I knew you worked until dark."

"I'm glad you called. I've been missing you a lot lately."

"Why I called is I just learned today that Stuart Leonard is running for county attorney. They're having an organization meeting Saturday for his campaign committee. I'm planning on attending and I thought you might be interested also."

"He'd make a great county attorney," Larry replied. "If it wasn't for him I wouldn't be able to see you and Vanessa on my days off. Bob was going to let me have both Saturday and Sunday off this weekend so maybe I will go to that. How about if I picked you up around nine-thirty Saturday morning?"

"Larry, we've never been in public together since we separated. This could really get the town talking," Libby chuckled.

"It's about time they said something good about me for a change," Larry replied. "I need to change my reputation. It's no fun being known as 'The Town Bad Boy'."

❧

That Saturday Larry and Libby Reynolds walked self-consciously into the meeting room of the Downtowner just as Jessica Mooney took the podium. "I'd like to welcome everyone to the meeting today," she began. "Although some of us may have never met, I'm sure we will be close friends by the time the election is over. We are bound together by one common belief and goal: Stuart

Leonard is the best qualified person for the Little Big Horn County Attorney Post."

With those words the entire group burst into loud applause and cheers. Stuart rose and raised his right hand for silence. "Thank you all for your support. I promise that if I am elected I will not let you down."

"I have listed some things that need to be done between now and election day," Jessica explained after Stuart returned to his seat. "I'll pass a sheet of paper around with the tasks and a tentative timetable. Please sign your name and telephone number beside the task and the times you could work."

When the sheet got around to Larry he studied it carefully and then shook his head. "Since I work six days a week from dawn to dusk there's no way I can help," he whispered to his estranged wife.

"I'm sure they'll understand, just as long as Stuart has your vote."

Larry's face turned glum. "I haven't registered to vote yet and there is only a couple days left to get that done. I've never voted before in my life. I never thought one vote would count for anything before."

"You'd better run, not walk, to the clerk's office first thing Monday morning and get that done," Libby whispered. "It's a good thing the courthouse is right across the street from where you're working."

Libby turned her attention back to the sheet now in front of her. Word Processing Needed Every Afternoon From 4:00-5:00. *That's something I can do,* she thought. *I've spent enough time in the campus computer center typing papers. In fact, I'm getting pretty good at it.*

Libby quickly signed her name and number, and passed

the sheet to the middle-aged lady sitting beside her.

When the meeting was over Larry invited Libby to the hotel cafe for a sandwich. After Larry had placed his order for a french dip and Libby ordered a club sandwich, they turned their attention back to each other.

"You know, Libby, this was the first time I've ever felt really accepted in the adult world. Even though I am a complete novice at least I feel like I am working for a worthwhile goal instead of just hanging out somewhere."

"I'm really looking forward to doing the typing on Jessica's computer. They say her system is as sophisticated as those used in most law offices. This could be good experience for me."

Larry studied his wife. She was a totally different woman from the scared girl who had to call the police to protect her from his cruelty. She was now sporting a new hairdo and had learned to use makeup wisely. By working with Pam Summer, she had modeled or sold enough clothes that she now had an entire wardrobe of Fashions by Rachel. However, these superficial changes were far less important than the inner strides his wife had made. *In a few weeks Libby will have completed her paralegal course and will be working in some law firm. I hope I can make that much of a change in my life.*

"A penny for your thoughts," Libby said as Larry's silence became almost deafening.

"I was just thinking about how lovely you are, and how much I like the changes in you," he admitted as he reached across the table and took her hand. "I hope someday I can earn your love and respect."

"You have made a good beginning," Libby assured him. "But we both need time to grow up before we can put our family back together again."

"How well I know," Larry replied. "Like we said before, we have to start dating all over again. However, that's been kind of hard with the long hours I've been working." He paused a moment before continuing. "How about a date tomorrow morning?"

"But it's Sunday," Libby protested. "Ever since we separated, I've been going to Edith's church. It somehow gives me enough strength to get through another week."

Larry smiled and a twinkle sparked each eye. "I know tomorrow's Sunday. That's why I asked. Would you accompany me to church tomorrow?"

❧

Libby and Larry arrived at church early the next morning and took seats in the back, reserved for parents with small children. "I use to think the roof of the church would fall in if I went in," Larry whispered.

"See, it didn't," Libby giggled back.

"I'm glad we have Vanessa with us. That gives us an excuse to sit in the far back. Otherwise, I'd feel like everyone was looking at us instead of the minister," Larry confided.

"I've always been shy and wanted to stay in the background but Edith, Teresa, and all the others have made me feel so welcomed here," Libby whispered as the organist began the prelude.

Pastor Rhodes based his sermon that Sunday on Second Corinthians, chapter five, verses seventeen through twenty (KJV): "New Life and Reconciliation."

> *Therefore if any man be in Christ, he is a new creature: old things are passed away; behold,*

all things are become new. And all things are of God, who hath reconciled us to himself by Jesus Christ, and hath given to us the ministry of reconciliation; To wit, that God was in Christ, reconciling the world unto himself, not imputing their trespasses unto them; and hath committed unto us the word of reconciliation. Now then we are ambassadors for Christ, as though God did beseech you by us: we pray you in Christ's stead, be ye reconciled to God.

How appropriate, thought Libby. *This just has to be God's seal of approval on the change in Larry and my reconciliation with him.*

Larry sat glued to his seat throughout the sermon. *Why, Pastor Rhodes seems to be speaking directly to me. Thank You, Lord,* he prayed silently, *for giving me a new life and reconciling me to my wife and daughter.*

Leaving the church, they stopped to chat with Roy and Edith Dutton and were soon joined by Bob and Nancy Harkness accompanied by Jay and Dawn.

"We are having dinner at my place," Nancy said as soon as there was a pause in the conversation. "Why don't you three join us?"

"Oh, I don't know," Larry hesitated. "We wouldn't want to impose."

"Nonsense," retorted Bob. "You're not imposing, you're invited."

"Well, okay, if you think it will be all right," Libby replied meekly.

Larry turned to Bob. "We'll follow you."

With that each one shook hands with Pastor Rhodes at

the door and headed for their vehicles. For the first time a church service had been a place of peace for Larry and not a place of boredom.

❧

When the Sunday dinner was over and the dishwasher loaded, the six grownups adjourned to the living room. Jay and Dawn disappeared outside to play while Vanessa slept soundly in her daddy's arms.

Edith looked over at the shy blond across the room. "Libby, I hope things have been going well for you."

"Oh, yes. Much better than I expected," Libby replied with satisfaction. "My only frustrations at the moment are my kitchen appliances; they keep breaking down. I guess I should expect that since I got most of them from the Thrift Store on Second Avenue."

Edith shook her head with understanding. "I know that can be plenty annoying."

"My toaster is on the blink and so is my electric coffeemaker." Libby paused and then sighed. "I can live with that, but yesterday my blender stopped as well. I need the blender to puree Vanessa's baby food. I guess I'll have to buy a new one, but that could be difficult on my budget."

"Well, why didn't you say something?" interjected Larry. "I'll buy you new ones the first thing tomorrow."

"No, Larry, don't do that," protested Edith. "I have a better idea. Why don't I throw a shower for you, Libby? This will give me an opportunity to be active again and I'll put a list of things you need on the invitation."

"There's a big disadvantage in eloping like you did two years ago," Nancy chuckled. "You miss out on bridal showers and you have to start housekeeping totally from scratch."

"Are you sure you want to go to that much trouble, Edith?" Libby asked.

"It's no trouble at all," Edith replied.

"I have a better idea," Nancy inserted. "Hold the shower here and I'll take care of the eats."

"Then it's settled," Edith stated as the others nodded their heads in agreement. "I'll try to arrange it for the middle of next week."

thirteen

Jay and Dawn were sitting on the living room floor watching TV cartoons when their mother returned from the supermarket. "Come on, kids," she pleaded. "Get with it. You promised to help me decorate the place. The guests will be arriving in less than three hours."

Jay reluctantly turned off the television, and he and Dawn stood on the sofa to hang the banner they had made for Libby's shower. The banner read: WE LOVE YOU, LIBBY AND VANESSA. Jay then left the remaining chores to Dawn and dashed out to play, mumbling, "This is girl stuff."

From the kitchen, Nancy heard the doorbell ring and Dawn shouting, "I'll get it!" And then, "Hi, Grandma. Come in and see the banner Jay and I made."

"Dawn, you remember Teresa Lennon, don't you?" Edith said as she motioned toward her companion. "She was kind enough to give me a ride over here."

"Oh, sure," Dawn replied. "I see her at church all the time."

Edith then turned her attention back to the banner. "It's very nice, Dawn. You and Jay did an excellent job. I'm sure Libby will love it."

"I'm in the kitchen, Edith," shouted Nancy who was unable to stop spreading the icing on the cake for fear it would harden too soon.

"I'll be right there to give you a hand," Edith replied. "I brought some extra help along with me."

Nancy greeted Teresa as she entered the kitchen. "I just had to give you a hand," Teresa said. "Libby is one of the major success stories of the Spouse Abuse Center and I want her to know how much we all appreciate her courage."

"What needs to be done?" Edith asked as she looked around the kitchen.

"How about you two making the relish tray? The carrots, celery, pickles, and olives are in the refrigerator."

Promptly at seven o'clock the doorbell began to ring almost incessantly. The room was soon filled to overflowing. Pam Summer came, as did Beth Slater, Jessica Mooney, Kim Packwood, and Mary Barker, wife of Libby's landlord. Patricia Reagan and Sonya Turner, volunteers at the Spouse Abuse Center, were bursting with excitement.

The table in the corner designated for gifts was stacked with packages of every size, shape, and color. Libby opened each gift with gratitude. Never before had she received so much love and attention at one time. Surprising enough, none of her gifts were duplicates. She was suspicious that Edith was behind that strange coincidence, but she did not dare ask.

After all the gifts were opened and the papers thrown away, Teresa turned her attention to Beth who was sitting beside her. "Beth, how are things going with you now that you've started the community college?"

"Classes are going great and I'm happier than I have ever been in my life," she replied. She paused before she continued. "However, I am also beginning to get worried. I just received a letter from a girlfriend in my hometown last week. She said that Mickey Kilmer had been kicked out of the Marine Corps and was back in town looking for me and Jeffy."

"He's Jeffy's father, isn't he?"

"Yes. But I don't want Mickey back in my life again. He's bad news. I'm afraid that one day he's going to show up here and try to take Jeffy from me."

"Just remember, Beth, you have a lot of friends in Rocky Bluff who will go to bat for you."

"Thanks, Teresa. I'll remember that."

"Nancy, I'd like to thank you and Edith for the beautiful shower and all of my friends here tonight for the wonderful gifts. You've all been just swell. I'll never forget what you've done for me, for Vanessa, for Larry. You've helped turn our lives around. Thank you and may God bless you."

As the guests were leaving, Jessica Mooney yelled, "Don't forget to vote tomorrow. Who do you want for county attorney?"

"Stuart Leonard!" came the response loud and clear.

❧

Election Day dawned sunny and crisp in Rocky Bluff. The anticipated blizzard did not materialize. Stuart Leonard's campaign staff was out in full force. Libby Reynolds was busy on the telephone arranging rides to the polls while Kim Packwood and Jessica Mooney drove voters to and from their polling sites.

During a midmorning break a thought flashed through Libby's mind. *What about Edith and Roy Dutton? Roy has limited his driving since he was diagnosed with diabetes and Edith has rarely been behind the wheel since her heart attack. Maybe I should give them a call.*

Libby dialed the Dutton residence and waited for the familiar answer. "Hello?"

"Hello, Edith. This is Libby. Thanks again for that

beautiful shower last night. I can't tell you how much I appreciate your efforts." Libby paused a moment before continuing. "I was wondering if you and Roy need a ride to the polls today. We have some critical local races being contested this time."

"Nancy and Bob were going to come by tonight, right before the polls close to give us a ride. They're all tied up with the construction of the new store. However, I'd like to get it done earlier, because we're both going to be pretty tired by eight o'clock."

"Kim and Jessica are providing rides to the polling places today. I can have one of them stop by and pick you up. What time would be convenient?"

"Any time is great," Edith replied, "but right after lunch would probably be the best. Then Roy would have time for his afternoon nap when he gets home. It's so kind of them to be doing this today."

"We're enjoying it," Libby replied. "I hadn't realized how much of a problem lack of transportation was for senior citizens. I've had to do without a car since Larry and I separated, but there's always a lot of younger people with cars going to the same places I am, or else I'm able to walk. But some of the people I've called are practically stranded every day."

Edith sighed with understanding. "It's difficult losing your independence once you've been active all your life. Roy and I are fortunate that we have family close by who are willing to take us anywhere we want to go, but many people have no family nearby."

Libby and Edith chatted for a few more minutes and then Libby excused herself to continue calling people from a list provided by the senior citizens' center.

By four-thirty that afternoon the list had been exhausted.

The three women, along with baby Vanessa went to Jessica's home to begin preparing for the victory celebration at eight o'clock. Stuart Leonard and his family and all those who helped on the election committee were going to sit glued to the local radio station and listen to the election results.

The women quickly prepared a finger buffet and began decorating the home. Jay and Dawn Harkness came early to help blow up and hang balloons and crepe paper streamers. They were elated to be included in the gala event, especially on a school night.

The first guests began to arrive promptly at eight o'clock. All speculated on the outcome of the election based on their own personal exit polls. After the living room was crowded with people Stuart and his wife arrived with their two children. Everyone was eager to talk with him, but he motioned for silence so they could hear the radio. The local radio talk show host was carrying on an annoying monologue to fill the time while the ballots were being counted. At nine-thirty a telephone call interrupted the noisy chatter of the celebration.

Everyone held their breath while Phil rushed to the phone. "Hello?"

"Hello," a businesslike voice responded. "Is Stuart Leonard there?"

"Just a moment please." Phil handed the phone to Stu who had quietly slipped to his side as soon as he heard the phone ring.

"Hello, this is Stuart Leonard."

"Hello Stu, Alex Snyder here at the election center. All precincts but one have reported in and I'm happy to inform you that you have been elected to the position of county attorney of Little Big Horn County by a two to one margin. Congratulations!"

Stuart gave the victory sign to the hushed group and everyone broke into cheers. Larry Reynolds had brought two bags of confetti for the occasion, much to the delight of the Harkness and Leonard children. "Speech! Speech!" echoed throughout the crowd.

Stuart raised his hand for silence. "I want to thank each of you for all your hard work. I couldn't have done it without you. I am really looking forward to serving as your county attorney and will do my utmost to enforce the laws of the great state of Montana. I would also like to announce my selection for staff. There is already a secretary in the office who will remain, but I am allowed to hire one paralegal. I have selected someone who through hard work and determination has proven that nothing is too difficult to conquer. She has put in many tireless hours working for my campaign."

Everyone looked from one person to another. Who among them had paralegal training? Few thought about the shy blond standing in the corner holding her baby. Their eyes returned to Stuart with anticipation.

"My selection is Libby Reynolds," he announced. "She will be graduating from the Paralegal Department at Rocky Bluff Community College December fourteenth with a straight A average. It is an honor to have her on my staff."

Libby stood in shocked silence. Never in her wildest dreams had she imagined herself as a paralegal for the Little Big Horn county attorney. Less than a year ago she felt that she deserved nothing more from life than to have her husband beat her, yet tonight she was entering on a promising new career.

Tears filled her eyes. "Thank you, thank you," she

whispered as she moved closer to Stuart who held out his hand for her to join him in the center of the room. "I'll try my best to live up to the confidence you're placing in me."

The entire group cheered, but the loudest cheers of all came from her handsome husband who had been standing beside her. Instead of living a life breaking the law, he had become an enthusiastic supporter of those enforcing it.

❧

The following Friday night as Roy and Edith were relaxing in front of the television set, Edith glanced over at Roy. Instead of his customary relaxed position, Roy's eyes were spacey and distance. He was perspiring and jittery. "Are you all right, Roy?" She asked.

Roy did not react, but continued as if he were not present in his body. "Roy, are you okay?" Edith said as she hurried to his side.

"Yeah, I guess. Pete was just here to see me."

Edith's face turned ashen. His son Pete had died more than two years before. She picked up Roy's wrist and felt his pulse pounding. She hurried to the phone and dialed for help.

"Emergency Services," an efficient voice responded. "How may I help you?"

"This is Edith Dutton. I need an ambulance right away. I think my husband is going into diabetic shock."

The dispatcher took Edith's address and advised her to remain calm and that an ambulance was on its way. Within minutes she could hear the sirens approaching and saw the reflections of the red lights. She flung the front door open as the paramedics appeared with a gurney. They immediately took a sample of blood from Roy's finger and placed a drop on a stick that they stuck into a small gray box.

"How low is it?" Edith asked as she leaned closer to read the meter.

The medic reached into his bag and took out a gel-covered capsule. "Thirty-five. We have to get glucose into him immediately." He then broke the capsule open and forced the liquid down Roy's throat.

In a few minutes Roy began to respond. "Roy, let's get you onto the stretcher. We're going to take you to the hospital for a few tests. Your blood sugar's way out of balance."

Edith took her coat from the front closet and followed the gurney to the waiting ambulance. She watched as they loaded her husband in the back and then one of the paramedics helped her climb into the front. On the way to the hospital they radioed Doctor Brewer that they were in transit with one of his patients.

Events moved swiftly upon arrival at the emergency room. Roy was immediately surrounded by Doctor Brewer and two nurses. While he was being treated, Edith found a pay phone in the corner of the lobby and phoned her son.

"Hello, Bob," she said, unable to hide her urgency. "Could you come to the emergency room right away? Roy had another bad spell. I think he's going to be okay, but it was pretty touch and go for a while."

"I'll be right there, Mom," Bob responded as he motioned to Nancy to come with him.

By the time Bob and Nancy got to the hospital Roy had been taken to a semiprivate room and was resting comfortably. "Hello, Mom," Bob whispered as he tiptoed into the room. "How is he?"

"There's no need to whisper." Roy retorted. "I'm doing fine. Everyone just overreacted. They're going to keep me here overnight and then I can go home in the morning."

Bob went over to his bed and took his hand. "I'm glad to hear that," he said. "If it's all right with you, can I take Mother home so she can get some rest?"

"Please do," Roy chuckled. "She looks more tired than I do. Just remember to have someone here to get me first thing in the morning."

"Don't worry. I'll be here," Bob promised. "Now get some rest and we'll see you in the morning."

❧

That weekend Roy and Edith remained home and rested. Nancy stopped by and prepared Sunday dinner for them. The next Tuesday morning the phone rang. Edith was greeted by a cheerful voice. "Hello, Mrs. Dutton. This is Barbara Hall, the head of United Charities. Is Roy available?"

"Just a moment, please."

Roy slowly raised his reclining chair and walked to the kitchen phone. "Hello."

"Hello, Roy. This is Barbara Hall. I'm pleased to inform you that at the United Charities Committee meeting last night we voted to increase the allocations to the Crisis Center. We decided to hire a full-time coordinator. Would you be willing to accept the position?"

Roy paused. Suddenly he realized that his desires were in direct conflict with reality. "Of course, I'd like nothing better than to accept," he replied dejectedly. "But now that I have diabetes I am unable to do so. It wouldn't be fair to the community if I took the position. But may I recommend someone else?"

"We're open for any suggestions," Barbara replied. "We hope to find someone who's experienced in the area of crisis intervention."

"I know just the man for the job," Roy stated. "He managed the Crisis Center by himself for several months a couple years ago when my son was killed. He drives a Western States Bus between here and Spokane, Washington. If it's a livable wage I'm sure he'll be interested."

"Sounds perfect. What's his name?"

"His name is Dan Blair. Just a moment and I'll give you his number." Roy thumbed through the listed of frequently called numbers in front of him. "Here it is. Seven eight nine, two one seven one."

"Thank you for your help and for all your years of service," Barbara replied. "Your recommendation is good enough for us. Dan Blair is our man."

❧

Eight o'clock on December fourteenth, friends and family members of Rocky Bluff Community College students gathered in the fieldhouse for the fall commencement ceremony. Edith was there with Bob and Nancy, while Roy stayed home to rest. Teresa was there grinning from ear to ear. Libby was one of the major success stories of the Spouse Abuse Center. *It's times like this that makes it all worthwhile,* she told herself.

Beside Teresa sat Beth Slater holding her two-and-a-half-year-old son. *If Libby can do it so can I,* she thought. *I can make it through the secretarial course.*

Proudest of all was Larry Reynolds who sat with his parents and his younger brother. Suddenly the school band began to play "Pomp and Circumstance" and the audience rose to their feet while the graduates slowly filed in. There was Libby, sixth from the end. Her face was serious and intent like her fellow graduates, but she winked at Larry as she passed his row.

How could I possibly have abused such a lovely, intelligent woman? Larry scolded himself. *I can hardly wait for Bob to get the store open so he can pay me a living wage. Then Libby and I and Vanessa can live together as a family again. I'm so delighted with the change in her. Only God could have produced such a miracle.*

fourteen

"Jim, be careful," Jean gasped as the car began fishtailing down the highway.

Jim Thompson took his foot from the gas pedal and began to steer in the direction of the skid. Fortunately no cars were approaching in the other lane. The Thompson car slid back and forth across the road for another fifty yards before Jim had it under control again.

"I certainly didn't expect roads like this," Jim exclaimed as he wiped the sweat from his brow. "The weather was perfect when we left Chamberland."

Jean breathed a sigh of relief. "I'm sure glad we have Gloria fastened in her car seat. I don't think she realized anything happened. I know it's early, but let's stop in Lincoln for the night. It's not worth the risk to go any farther. Roger's Pass could be a real bear."

"We promised Bob we'd be in late tonight so we'd have all day tomorrow to help him set up the displays, but they'll have to go it alone," Jim said as he turned off at the Sleepy Eye Motel. "He still has three days before his grand reopening so we can work like crazy to help once we get there."

❧

Bob and Nancy Harkness along with Larry Reynolds had spent twelve hours per day at the store since the first of the year. First there were the walls to paint and then the display cases needed to be put together. Nancy's big day came when the new computer system arrived. Not only was she going to have new hardware to work with, but she had entirely new software.

As she poured over the manuals and did the trial exercises, Larry was drawn more and more to what was happening on the monitor. "Nancy, I know you're too busy right now, but sometime I'd sure like to learn more about computers."

"I'd be a poor teacher," Nancy chuckled. "I'm having trouble enough trying to get this supposedly easy program functioning before we open the doors for business." Nancy thought for a moment. "I think Paul's Computer Store gives introductory classes every so often. Why don't you take your coffee break and walk down the block and ask them?"

"I think I'll do that," Larry replied as he reached for his coat. "Computers were just getting started when I was in high school, but at the time I thought it would be too much work to learn. Now they look absolutely fascinating."

Twenty minutes later Larry opened the front door and stomped the snow from his shoes on the mat. His cheeks were pink from the biting wind. "Paul has a good thing going at his store. There is a small classroom in the back and introductory classes will be meeting for the next four Wednesday nights, but the only problem is. I don't have fifty dollars. My car insurance is due this month."

Bob looked up from the box of screwdrivers that he was trying to arrange on the shelf. "Larry, you've more than kept up your end of the bargain. You've been putting in some pretty long hours working at minimum wage. I told you I'd put you on regular salary as soon as we opened the store. Obviously, that's just days away. But as a bonus I'd like to pay your tuition for that class. I'll go down and talk to Paul a little later and get things set up for you."

"Thanks Bob. You don't know how much I appreciate this."

Bob slapped Larry on the shoulder and snickered. "Since you'll be making a living wage I bet you'll be getting anxious to get a place of your own and out of our cramped basement."

"You were reading my mind," Larry replied. "I was thinking about a place of my own not because your basement room is small, but because I'm planning to ask Libby to rejoin me. I want us to live together again as a family. Just watching you and Nancy with the kids makes me homesick for my own family."

❧

Libby walked up the steps of the courthouse. Her high heels echoed down the hallway as they hit the marble floor. She paused in front of the Little Big Horn County Attorney's office and took out a key. Opening the door, the enormity of her job enveloped her. The desk before her was her desk, complete with a picture of little Vanessa in the corner. The computer was there for her sole usage. *If there ever was a miracle, it's plain and simple here: me doing research for a county attorney. I could never have done it on my own.*

"Hi, Libby," a friendly voiced called from the next room. "I've been waiting for you. When you get settled come into my office, I have a search I want you to do on the online legal database."

"I'll be right there," Libby replied as she hung her coat in the closet and put her purse in the drawer beside her desk.

"What can I help you with?" Libby asked as she stepped

into Stuart Leonard's modest office. "Another heavy case?"

"It sure is," Stu replied. "I'll need all the help I can get. I'm glad you have the latest training available in telecommunications. I missed all of that when I was in law school. Would you dial up the legal database and find everything you can on this subject?"

He handed her a scrap of paper with several terms scribbled on them. She smiled at the nearly illegible handwriting that she was beginning to learn to decipher. "I'll get right on it," she promised as she hurried back to her office and flipped the switch to her computer.

❧

Nancy and Bob Harkness had just ordered a quick sandwich at the Corner Grill when Stuart Leonard walked in. "Hi, Stuart," Bob said as the county attorney passed their table. "Care to join us for lunch?"

"Sure," Stu replied as he pulled up a chair. "Beats eating alone."

Stu motioned to the waitress. She immediately returned to the table with a menu in hand. He quickly glanced over the menu and said, "I'll have a ham sandwich on rye bread, please, with a cup of split pea soup."

"Thank you, sir," she smiled as she took the menu from his hand.

Stu turned his attention back to the Harknesses with a twinkle in his eye. "I've noticed my employee is showing a lot of interest in your employee."

"They've been having lunch together nearly every noon," Nancy replied with satisfaction. "And even better than that, they've been in church together every Sunday since Thanksgiving. I think things are beginning to come together for them."

"Larry mentioned to me the other day that he was looking for a two-bedroom house or apartment. It wouldn't surprise me at all to see a complete reunion within a month or two. They're both making a decent wage now."

"When I went before the judge to request Larry's restraining order be lifted I did so with a great deal of misgiving," Stu admitted. "However, Larry is proving that he is worthy of our trust. After seeing so many young people throw their lives away it's good to finally see a success story. Hopefully, other troubled teens will notice from their examples that there's always hope that life can get better, regardless of how bad things appear at the time."

❧

The next day the phone rang in the Little Big Horn County Attorney's Office. The secretary promptly answered and then turned to Libby who was busy inputting data into the computer. "It's for you."

"Hello, this is Libby Reynolds."

"Hi, Lib, I'm sorry to bother you at work," Beth Slater replied. "I have some good news and I just couldn't wait to tell you."

Libby swirled in her chair, "That's okay. I need a momentary break. What's going on?"

"I got my first test back at the college and I actually got an A. I've never had an A before, except for maybe third grade gym class," Beth exclaimed excitedly. "I know it's old hat to everyone else, but I always thought I was too stupid to learn much."

"Beth, I knew you could do it. If I could do, it so can you. Have you told Edith Dutton yet?"

"I want to see the look on her face when I tell her." Beth hesitated. "In fact, I think I'll take my paper over and show it to her. As soon as Jeffy wakes up from his nap I'll put him in the sled and walk over there. None of this would have been possible without her. And to think it all started with a desperate call to the Crisis Center."

❧

Jim and Jean waited until late morning before they left the Sleepy Eye Motel. They wanted to give plenty of time for the road crews to clear the pass. The remainder of their trip was uneventful.

"I hope your mom's not in bed when we get there," Jim said as he and Jean reached the outskirts of Rocky Bluff.

"I can see her now," Jean replied as her eyes held a distant gaze. "She's lying on the sofa in her robe watching TV and listening for every car that comes down the street. She could never sleep until she knew her family was home and safe and sound. Particularly if we were traveling during the winter."

Just as Jean had expected, the faint flicker of the TV was seen through the drawn blinds of the Dutton residence. Jean hurriedly unstrapped the sleeping Gloria from her car seat while Jim hurried to the trunk to get the luggage. The biting winter air stimulated their weary bodies. The front door flung open just as Jean reached the top step.

"Jean, honey, it's so good to see you," Edith exclaimed as she gave her daughter a hug. "How was your trip?"

"Tiring." Jean laid the baby on the floor while she took off her coat. Her first instinct was to hand the baby to her mother, but she thought better of it. Gloria was getting to be a chunk and Edith's arm strength had been greatly weakened since her heart attack.

"How's my baby?" Edith queried as she admired her dark-haired granddaughter lying on the floor.

"She's doing great. She got a little tired of her car seat

for a while this morning, but she soon went back to sleep. All considering, she traveled extremely well."

Jean quickly unbundled the baby and sat with her mother on the sofa while Jim brought the luggage in from the car and carried them to the guest room. "How's Roy been doing?" she inquired.

"He's sleeping now," Edith explained as she fought back a yawn. "Basically he has his good days and he has his bad days. However, I'm afraid that the bad days are becoming more and more frequent."

"I'll do what I can to help while I'm here," Jean assured her and then quickly changed the subject. "How's Bob coming with the store?"

"It's been a long haul, but he's just about finished. I think he only has a couple more shelves to price and fill and he'll be ready to roll."

"He'd like to have Roy and me along with you and Jim there serving cake and coffee during the three-day reopening. He's put a lot of money into advertising the event, so if the weather cooperates we should have a good turnout."

"I hear he's hired Larry Reynolds full time now. How's that been working out?"

"Unbelievably well," Edith assured her daughter. "Larry has gotten so involved that he's even taking computer classes to help with the business part of the store. Bob has been an outstanding influence on him."

Jean giggled. "My former self-centered, money-hungry brother is now the community role model. Miracles do happen."

❧

The sun shone warmly as Bob Harkness unlocked the front door of the *new* Harkness Hardware Store on the day of the grand reopening. Jean dropped Gloria at an old high school friend's home for the day and then drove Jim, Edith, and Roy to the store. Edith and Roy made themselves comfortable at the refreshments table by the door while Jean and Nancy finished putting the finishing touches on the serving table. Everything was arranged perfectly. The day they'd worked toward for so long could begin.

Bob glanced out the window as he arranged the supplies under the front counter. The delivery van from Specialty Florist pulled to a stop. The driver jumped from the cab and opened the side door and took out a huge bouquet of flowers and entered the store.

"Where would you like these?" he asked Bob.

Bob hurriedly surveyed the front of the store. "How about on this stand?" he replied. "Who are they from?"

"This one is from Rick at the bank," the delivery man replied as he set the bouquet on the stand. "But I have others."

He turned and hurried from his van with another bouquet with *Good Luck* written on its ribbon. "This one is from Warren Engelwood in Great Falls."

He went to the van again and returned with another. "This one is from Paul's Computer Store."

He hastened to his van and returned with still another. "Good luck, from Mr. and Mrs. Stuart Leonard."

Before he was finished twelve different bouquets lined the walls of the hardware store. Even the president of the Chamber of Commerce sent a congratulatory bouquet.

Nancy put her arm around Bob's waist and laid her head against his chest. Tears filled her eyes. "I never dreamed we'd have this much support. A few months ago it seemed like the entire community was against us, and now they're all behind us." She shrugged her shoulders and laughed.

"That's life in little town Montana."

Edith looked at Roy, who was obviously enjoying stuffing himself with refreshments. "Roy, remember your caloric intake and absolutely no sweets. I want to walk around and look over the new inventory. Will you be okay for a while?"

"Edith," Roy scolded, "you worry too much about me. Please go. I'll be fine."

As Edith walked around the new store, she marveled at the different tools and equipment farmers and ranchers used today. She saw very few farm implements that were familiar when she and George ran the store. *I hope all of these new devices help take some of the backbreaking drudgery out of farm work,* she mused.

She glanced around the store and spied Roy talking to Dan Blair and hurried to greet him. The last time she saw Dan was at her and Roy's wedding reception.

"Dan, so nice to see you again. How have you been?"

Dan extended his hand. "Edith, it's great to see you again. I was just telling Roy that Barbara Hall of United Charities has offered me the position of full-time director of the Crisis Center."

"And he accepted," Roy chimed in.

"Yes, thanks to Roy's outstanding recommendation, Barbara offered the job to me. It doesn't pay as much as the bus company, but at least I'll be home every night."

Just then a crisp breeze of winter air hit their faces as the front door opened. All turned to greet Beth Slater as she walked by carrying little Jeffy.

"Oh, Beth do come and meet Dan Blair, the new director of the Crisis Center," Edith said. "Dan, this is Beth Slater and her son Jeffy."

"Pleased to meet you, Beth," Dan said graciously as he

reached out to shake her hand.

"And I, you," she replied with a smile. "I'm an alumnus of the Crisis Center," she chuckled. "I don't know what I would have done without Edith's and Roy's assistance. I'm glad that Roy's passing the directorship to such capable hands."

Dan grinned as his face flushed. "Thank you for those kind words. I'm certainly going to try to live up to Roy's faith in me."

"Well, Beth," Edith broke in. "Little Jeffy is his usual well-behaved self. It must be fun having him learning how to talk. It doesn't seem like any time at all since he was just a tiny one in your arms." Edith then turned her attention to the young man beside her. "Dan, Beth just enrolled in the secretarial school at the Community College."

"That's tremendous. I'm sure you'll do well." Dan could not take his eyes off Beth's sparkling blue eyes. "There's always room for one more secretary in Rocky Bluff. Perhaps after you finish the course you can help me type the Crisis Center's weekly reports. My typing ability is pretty limited."

"I'd be happy to," Beth smiled. "Well, if you folks will excuse me, I'd like to take a moment to congratulate Bob and Nancy. They've worked so hard on this place. Then I better take Jeffy home and put him to bed. It's way past his afternoon nap time."

"Stop by the house and see us sometime," Edith invited. "Our doors are always open."

"I'll do that," Beth assured her. "It's good to see you again." The young woman turned her attention to Edith's husband. "Roy, I do hope you get better. I'll remember you in my prayers." Beth then paused as she turned to her new acquaintance. "Dan, nice meeting you and if I ever master the art of typing, I promise to help with those weekly reports."

As the front door closed behind Beth, Edith turned to Roy. "There goes one sweet lady."

"That she is," he agreed as his thoughts flew back through the last few months. "She's come so far from the scared little girl I met two years ago."

"She seems like a very nice person. I'm surprised I've never seen her before. Who's her husband?" Dan asked.

"She's not married." Edith replied. "She was very much in love with her fiancé, but when she became pregnant he beat her and left town. That was more than two years ago and she hasn't seen or heard from him since, not that it makes any difference. As far as she's concerned it's all over between them, and Beth is better off without him."

"She's too lovely for anyone to abandon," Dan sighed.

fifteen

"Libby, now that the store is open again Bob gave me a substantial raise. It's time for me to find a place of my own," Larry said as the young couple relaxed in Libby's small apartment the week following the reopening.

Tears welled in Libby's eyes as she took his hand. "I'm so proud of you, Larry. Everything's turning out better than I could ever have imagined."

"Libby, would you be willing to come back and live with me? I could look for a house or apartment big enough for the three of us and possibly someday, the four of us."

Libby hesitated. She had been dreaming about this day for months, but now that it had happened she was speechless. She had gotten used to an independent life-style, would she be able to readjust to married life once again? The she looked into Larry's deep, intense eyes. *How can I possibly hesitate? Here is the same boy I fell in love with more than two years ago who has matured into one of the kindest men in Rocky Bluff. My cup runneth over.*

"Yes. . .of course," she stammered.

Larry took her into his arms. "You'll never regret this. I promise. I'll be the best husband and father in the county."

"You'll have to be," Libby giggled. "After all, you're married to the paralegal for the county attorney."

"I've been watching the paper for rental units and there just aren't many available," Larry admitted dejectedly.

"I don't know how soon I'll be able to find a place for all of us."

"Rumor has it that a two-bedroom apartment is going to be available here in the Forest Grove Apartments the middle of February. But I'm not sure which one it is."

Larry brightened. "I'll check with your manager in the morning and see if we can rent that one. What apartment is he in? Not having to rent a truck would sure make moving day a lot easier."

"He's in number seventeen. . .the end unit. His name is Ron and his wife's name is Mary. They have a real cute place." Libby hesitated before she spoke again. "Larry, there's something else I'd really like to do before we become a family again." Libby leaned against his chest with his arm wrapped around her. "I'd like to renew our wedding vows. This time we can make our promise before God and really mean it."

"That's a great idea." Larry's voice was firm with conviction. "I'll add one more thing on my list to do. I'll contact Pastor Rhodes and see if he would conduct a simple ceremony in the church sanctuary." Larry stroked her cheek softly as he gazed into her blue eyes. "Libby, you'll never regret this."

The pair continued their discussion far into the night, forgetting that they both had to be up early for work. At midnight, Libby began to yawn and they bid each other good night. Neither one slept well that night. This time it was joy and excitement that kept them awake, not frustration.

❧

The next morning Libby sleepily dragged herself out of bed, got herself and Vanessa dressed, and hurried Vanessa to the daycare center. Soon she would have someone to wake up with and help her with her early morning chores. No longer would she have to sit alone over her morning cup of coffee.

During her morning break she dialed a familiar number.

"Hello?"

"Hello, Edith. This is Libby. How are you and Roy? I haven't seen you since the store's reopening."

"We're doing fine," Edith assured her. "But we're not doing as much as we'd like."

"I have some great news," Libby continued excitedly. "Larry and I are going to get back together just as soon as we can find a place to live."

Edith's eyes sparkled as she remembered the broken young woman and baby she had taken to the Spouse Abuse Center more than a year before. "I'm so happy for you both. You're an encouragement to other young people to tough it out through the hard times."

"Larry's going to talk to Pastor Rhodes about using the sanctuary of the church to renew our wedding vows."

"Libby, that's perfect. Would you let Nancy and me plan a reception afterwards in your honor?"

The young woman hesitated. She had never had a regular wedding and reception before. She and Larry had eloped to Coeur D'Alene, Idaho, two years before, been married in the "Lover's Chapel," and had spent the night in the Pink Flamingo Getaway. "Oh, Edith. I don't deserve anything that nice," she muttered. "People have been so good to us."

"We'd love to do it," Edith assured her. "This time I want to make sure you have a memorable fresh beginning. Start thinking about some of your friends that you would like to have attend."

Libby then glanced at the clock over her head. "Oh, dear. I better get back to work. I'm in the middle of some pretty heavy research for Stu."

❧

That afternoon, Larry called Pastor Rhodes at the church study and asked him if he would conduct a renewal of wedding vows ceremony for Libby and him.

"I'd be delighted to," Pastor Rhodes assured him. "However, since you did not have a traditional wedding before, I would like to meet with both you and Libby for a couple of counseling sessions. I'd like to cover some of the basic marriage principles that I discuss with all engaged couples."

"That seems reasonable," Larry replied. "We want to make sure everything goes right this time. Not too many people get a second chance like we have."

"How about you and Libby coming to my study Saturday at two o'clock? We could make specific plans as to date and time then," Pastor Rhodes suggested as he thought back through the changes, both the good and the bad, he had seen in Larry from the time he first met him ten years ago until today.

❧

That evening after work when Larry stopped at the Forest Grove Apartments he found the manager, Ron, extremely accommodating.

"Yes, Larry, apartment twenty will be available February fifteenth. The tenants are moving out the first and we need a couple weeks to clean and paint the walls. The carpeting is getting plenty worn so we thought this would be the best time to replace it. Are you interested in renting it?"

"I sure am," Larry assured him. "Do I need to put down a deposit to hold it?"

"Normally there would be a three hundred dollar cleaning deposit but since Libby already lives in the complex it won't be necessary. Just pay us two weeks' rent for the remainder of February when you move in."

"I'm sorry I can't show you the apartment until the current tenant moves out, but I can show you this one. They're exactly the same except the rooms are reversed."

Ron led Larry through his immaculate two-bedroom apartment. "Your wife has excellent decorating tastes," Larry observed.

"That she does," Ron agreed as he grinned at his wife who was at the dining room table helping her son with his homework. "She could make a storeroom into a work of art."

Larry could hardly wait to get to Libby's apartment to share the news of the day. She was busy getting Vanessa ready for bed when Larry knocked on her door. She hurried to the door and flung it open. "Come in, Larry. I'm glad you're here in time to say goodnight to Vanessa before she goes to bed."

Larry took off his coat, laid it over the arm of the sofa, and picked up his daughter. She was looking more like her mother with each passing day. Vanessa giggled as Larry began making faces at her as he held her gently in his arms.

"Don't get her too excited," Libby cautioned. "I want to get her to sleep tonight."

"Let me read a quick story to her before we put her to

bed. Does she have a favorite?"

"She seems to like the one about the kittens," Libby replied as she reached for a cardboard book on the shelf. "She likes to hear me try to imitate the kittens while she looks at the pictures."

Vanessa was soon asleep in her daddy's arms. Larry quietly laid the book back on the shelf and tiptoed into the bedroom. He laid her sleeping form in the crib and paused. He held his breath as she stirred and then rolled to her side and was fast asleep.

Libby watched from the bedroom doorway. *It is so important for little girls to have father figures to identify with. I'm so thankful Vanessa will now be able to grow up with her daddy to help guide and comfort her.*

Larry took Libby's hand and gently led her back to the living room sofa. "This has been one perfect day," he whispered.

Libby's eyes glistened. "Why? What has happened?"

"First I called Pastor Rhodes and he said he would be honored to help us renew our wedding vows. He would like us to come by the study next Saturday at two o'clock to set up the details and to have some basic marriage counseling."

"It's all so exciting," Libby replied. "When I called to tell Edith the good news she said she and Nancy wanted to have a reception for us. It's going to be like a regular church wedding which we didn't have the first time."

"That's not all," Larry interrupted. "I talked with your manager on my way over to see you. He said we could move into apartment number twenty on February fifteenth. He said we wouldn't be able to see that apartment until the current tenant moves out, but he showed me his apartment, which is just like it except the rooms are reversed. You were right. Those two-bedroom apartments are really nice."

Libby sat in silence for a moment before reacting. "Do you know what would be romantic?"

"Just being with you is romantic," Larry said as he pulled her closer to himself.

"You know what I mean," she snickered. "Wouldn't it be romantic to renew our wedding vows on Valentine's Day? The following day we could move into our new apartment."

"Sounds good to me. Let's suggest that to Pastor Rhodes Saturday," Larry replied. "Say, what all does Edith have in mind for the reception?"

"I don't know for sure but she wants us to make a list of friends we want to include. I haven't started the list yet, but I do know I want Beth Slater to be at the very top of that list. She's been there whenever I've needed a friend."

Larry took out a sheet of paper and began listing people with whom they'd like to share that happy day. Before they were through they were shocked that there were more than fifty friends and relatives listed. "Are you sure Edith is expecting a list this long?" Larry queried as he finished counting the names.

"She said the sky's the limit," Libby replied, wanting to share that happy day with the entire world. "She said she wanted to invite a few friends of their own as well. Especially those who work at the Crisis Center. Roy wants them to see one of their victory cases. She says they go a long time without seeing positive results, so our renewal of vows could be a real encouragement to them."

Larry shrugged his shoulders with delight. "The more

the merrier."

❧

February fourteenth, Nancy and Beth spent all day decorating the fellowship hall of the church with hearts and cupids among the red and white streamers. Edith worked a while in the morning and then brought Dawn by after school to put on the finishing touches. The Goody Bakery had designed a three-tier wedding cake that graced the center of the serving table. Everything was perfect.

Promptly at seven o'clock the wedding march began. Libby, dressed in a pale pink and white dress, started down the aisle on the arm of Roy Dutton. If ever there were a model father to help a young woman take the crucial steps toward a successful marriage, it was he.

Larry's face broke into a broad grin as he saw his wife begin the long descent down the aisle to the altar. The beautiful bride on the arm of a distinguished father-figure was an image from a story book.

The actual renewal of vows took only a few moments. Tears filled Libby's eyes. *The last time I said these words I didn't know what I was getting into, but it seemed like it would be fun. Tonight I know what I am getting into and I know we have to have God's help to make a marriage work.*

Larry and Libby moved easily through the crowd, accepting congratulations and expressions of good luck. They came face to face with Viola Tomkins, Grady Walker's secretary, whom Larry had scared that horrible day so long ago.

Neither spoke at first. Then Larry cleared his throat. "Forgive me, Viola, I'm truly sorry for what happened and that you had to witness such a terrible deed. I wasn't thinking straight."

With that Viola gave Larry a quick hug. "Oh, Larry," Viola exclaimed. "The important thing is that you're thinking straight now. The past is past."

"Thank you," he murmured as he turned to the woman at his side. "I'd like you to meet my wife, Libby."

Libby extended her hand. "I'm glad to meet you, Viola. Thank you for coming."

"I had to. The whole town is so happy for you and Larry. From the bottom of my heart, I wish you both the best."

"Excuse me," Larry interrupted. "I see the Mooneys and the Packwoods over there and I want to thank them for standing behind me at the court hearing."

Larry took his wife's hand and led her across the room. "Phil, Scott," Larry began. "Words can't express how much I appreciate what you two have done for me. You're the greatest."

"Not to worry, Larry. Now that we no longer have to contend with you, we can concentrate on the real criminals among us," Phil quipped to the amusement of all.

"Jessica, you remember the famous Larry Reynolds. Larry, my wife, Jessica."

"I'm delighted to see you again, Mrs. Mooney. We met at Stu Leonard's election headquarters. But Phil should have introduced me as infamous."

"You have rehabilitated yourself, Larry, and Rocky Bluff has dropped the "i" and "n" but kept the famous."

"That's true," chimed in Kim Packwood. "I hope you and Libby have a long and happy marriage."

"That goes double for me, too, Larry," Scott Packwood said as he shook Larry's hand.

"Your wedding dress is just gorgeous. Did you make it yourself?" asked Grady Walker's wife, Phyllis.

"Oh, no," Libby replied. "I could never do anything this nice. I had lots of help. Beth Slater chose the material and Pam Summer designed it. Edith introduced me to her former next-door neighbor, Beverly Short, who made it for me. Mrs. Short is an amazing woman. She's over seventy, but she does wonders with her fingers."

"I agree with you," Grady said. "We've known Bev Short all our lives. She made our daughter's wedding dress a few years ago. Libby, Phyllis, and I wish you and Larry all the best."

"Thank you, Grady. Coming from you that means so much to us."

Larry continued to move around the room greeting well-wishers, when he spied Amy Wallace, the Rocky Bluff High School nurse. Larry permitted himself to reminisce. *Beautiful Amy. She hasn't changed a bit. She's just as lovely now as she was when I was in high school. I had such a schoolboy crush on her back then. But so did half the male student body population.*

"Oh, Larry." It was Edith Dutton. "Please come here. I want you to meet someone." Larry moved to Edith's side. "Larry, this is Grace Blair and her son, Dan."

"It's a pleasure to meet you both," Larry said as he and Dan shook hands.

Edith continued. "Dan is the new director of the Crisis Center."

"Oh, yeah. I remember reading about that. Congratulations. That center is doing a great job. My wife can attest to that."

"Nice of you to say so. Mother and I hope that you and

Libby will be very happy."

"With friends like these," Larry waved his arm around the room, "how could we not?"

A hush came over the room as Roy Dutton loudly tapped a spoon against a decanter.

"Folks, could I have your attention, please. Will everyone fill their cup with some of the delicious punch my daughter-in-law Nancy Harkness made. I want to propose a toast to the bride and groom."

There was a mad dash to the punch bowl and some good-natured shoving that caused no little amount of punch to be spilled on the carpet. Pastor Rhodes grinned as he remembered it was Bob and Nancy's turn to clean the church that week. Finally the room settled down and all the guests faced Roy, who now had Larry and Libby by his side.

"To the bride and groom!" Roy shouted as he raised his cup. "May the good Lord richly bless and keep them both."

Shouts of "Hear-hear," "all right," "you bet," and "God bless you," filled the room. And then "Speech, speech" was followed by a thunderous applause.

"I don't know what to say. You've all been so wonderful," Larry began. "I just thank God that I live in Rocky Bluff with all of you wonderful people. I feel like I have been handed a second chance at life and I promise you I will devote the rest of my life to making my wife and baby happy. Thank you all."

Libby was too overcome with emotion to speak and could only wave to the cheering and understanding crowd. As Larry and Libby stood facing their guests, a familiar figure made his way to the front. He stood before Larry with his left arm behind his back as though concealing something.

"Coach Watson!" Larry shouted with undisguised glee. Todd Watson was coach of the Rocky Bluff High School basketball team. Not since that horrible day in Larry's life when Todd Watson entered the principal's office and led Larry away after Edith had disarmed him had Larry seen his old mentor.

Grady Walker also came to the front of the room and stood beside Todd.

"Larry, Grady and I have something for you. You would have received this on your graduation night if you'd been there. We've been saving it for the right moment and we can't think of a moment more right than this one." With that, Todd brought his left arm from behind his back and handed Larry a beautiful trophy. "There's an inscription on it. Won't you read it for us?" Grady asked.

Larry took the trophy with trembling hands and began to read: "To Larry Reynolds," he read aloud. "Rocky Bluff High School's Most Valuable Player Award. Montana State Class A Basketball Championship Game, Billings, Montana, March fifteenth. . ." Larry couldn't finish. It was all too much for him. So many good things had happened to him in such a short period of time. He buried his head in his hands and cried like a baby.

Libby threw her arms around him as his mother and father rushed to his side. The crowd once again applauded. There were few dry eyes among them.

When Larry regained his composure, Bob Harkness asked the Reynolds family to pose for a family photo to memorialize the happy occasion. Larry, Libby, and Donald and Frances Reynolds stood side by side as Bob focused and snapped the picture.

"Wait a minute, Bob. I want Ryan in this too," said Larry. "Ryan," he yelled. "Where are you?"

There was no answer.

"I think Ryan's among the missing along with Jay and Dawn," Bob observed with a chuckle.

The three were on a self-appointed mission in front of the church where Larry had parked his car. They were preparing Larry's car for the honeymoon getaway. Dawn stepped back to admire her handiwork. With a bar of white soap, she had drawn a heart on the passenger's side door with an arrow running through it. Inside the heart she had added "Larry and Libby."

Ryan had been busy collecting soda pop cans for days and stringing them together. He tied the noise makers to the rear bumper laughing all the while. "Boy, that's going to make a lot of noise," he giggled with self-satisfaction.

"It sure will," agreed Jay as he busied himself soaping "JUST MARRIED AGAIN" across the rear window.

"I wish my dog, Ralph, could be here. I'd hide him in the back seat. That would shake them up."

Finishing their happy chore, the children hid in the shrubbery by the church building to watch the fun when the bride and groom emerged.

Meanwhile, after the toast and the presentation the crowd began to mill around again in the fellowship hall. Dan Blair spotted Beth Slater across the room. Little by little he inched his way in her direction trying not to be too obvious. Finally, he was beside her.

"Hello, Beth," he began politely. "I'm Dan Blair. We met at the reopening of Harkness Hardware Store."

"Hi, Dan," she replied cheerfully. "I remember you. You're now the full-time director of the Crisis Center."

"You do have a good memory," he chided.

"How could I possibly forget anyone who works for the Crisis Center. That was how I met Edith and got my life straightened around."

"She and Roy have been an inspiration to many people," Dan reminded her. "Look how much they've done for Larry and Libby."

"That couple proves that with God's help nothing can stand in the way of true love." Beth's eyes became distant. "But in my case it's doubtful if love is possible since I already have a child."

"Beth, you were the one who caught the bridal bouquet," Dan grinned as he observed the flowers in her hand. "Isn't that proof enough that love can be possible with or without a child? Give it time. A year ago Libby would never have though she would be where she is today."

❧

"What are they doing in there?" asked Dawn from her hiding place in the shrubbery.

"I don't know," Ryan whispered. "Why don't you go and see?"

"Okay, I'll be right back," Dawn mumbled as she dashed up the steps of the church. She entered the church and turned to go to the fellowship hall when she heard a loud commotion as the reception party began to leave. Flying out of the church and back to her hiding place she yelled, "Here they come!"

The guests broke into squeals of laughter as they saw Larry's car. "Ryan!" Larry yelled in mock despair. "Just wait until I get back."

From the safety of their hiding places, the three children shook with laughter.

At last it was time to go, and Larry and Libby waved to the crowd as they sped off trailing five feet of soda pop cans noisily behind them.

Edith turned to Roy. "The Lord works in mysterious ways His wonders to perform."

"Amen to that," said Dan Blair as he squeezed Beth Slater's hand.

A Letter To Our Readers

Dear Reader:

In order that we might better contribute to your reading enjoyment, we would appreciate your taking a few minutes to respond to the following questions. When completed, please return to the following:

Rebecca Germany, Editor
Heartsong Presents
P.O. Box 719
Uhrichsville, Ohio 44683

1. Did you enjoy reading *Contagious Love*?
   - ❑ Very much. I would like to see more books by this author!
   - ❑ Moderately

   I would have enjoyed it more if ___________

   ____

2. Are you a member of *Heartsong Presents*? Yes No
   If no, where did you purchase this book? _________

   ____

3. What influenced your decision to purchase this book? (Check those that apply.)

   ❑ Cover ❑ Back cover copy

   ❑ Title ❑ Friends

   ❑ Publicity ❑ Other _______________

4. On a scale from 1 (poor) to 10 (superior), please rate the following elements.

___Heroine ___Plot

___Hero ___Inspirational theme

___Setting ___Secondary characters

5. What settings would you like to see covered in *Heartsong Presents* books?

____

____

6. What are some inspirational themes you would like to see treated in future books?________________

____

____

7. Would you be interested in reading other *Heartsong Presents* titles? ❑ Yes ❑ No

8. Please check your age range:

❑ Under 18 ❑ 18-24 ❑ 25-34

❑ 35-45 ❑ 46-55 ❑ Over 55

9. How many hours per week do you read? ________

Name ____

Occupation ____________________________________

Address ______________________________________

City ______________ State _____ Zip __________

Introducing New Authors

Kathleen Yapp

___*A New Song*—As Serena Lawrence contemplates her uncertain musical future, the future of her heart becomes center stage. With Steve at her side, will Serena sing a new song? HP70 $2.95

Dianne L. Christner

___*Proper Intentions*—On the precipice of the nineteenth century, Beaver Creek needs a new church to reach out to those in need, and a man of proper intentions to claim the heart of a beautiful, faithful woman. HP80 $2.95

Page Winship Dooly

___*Heart's Desire*—Cole Wilder agrees to escort Hannah to her aunt's home in Missouri. Will their journey end in a handshake or will they realize in time their hearts' desire? HP84 $2.95

Loree Lough

__*Pocketful of Love*—Out of their sorrow a friendship develops, and the possiblility of love. However, vengeful enemies and jealous rivals determine to destroy the bloom of happiness Elice and Cabot have found in each other's arms. HP86 $2.95

Send to: Heartsong Presents Reader's Service
P.O. Box 719
Uhrichsville, Ohio 44683

Please send me the items checked above. I am enclosing $________(please add $1.00 to cover postage and handling per order. OH add 6.25% tax. NJ add 6% tax.).
Send check or money order, no cash or C.O.D.s, please.

To place a credit card order, call 1-800-847-8270.

NAME ______________________________

ADDRESS ______________________________

CITY/STATE ____________________ ZIP __________